This story is mostly fiction, and the characters are fictitious, but there is one exception. Ben, the owner of the small hardware store featured in this story. He was a great friend to many who knew him back in 1957.

It was in 1972, some fifteen years after the fictional event told in this story, that South Australia's Tumby Bay jetty was about to be demolished. However, thanks to the unrelenting picketing organised by the townsfolk, demolition never happened.

This mural, painted by Martin Schlick @Masher Designs, sits on the Tumby Bay foreshore, not far from the jetty, and it celebrates the colony of Leafy Seadragons that still live beneath it.

Smile Time Books are written for anyone who enjoys a feel-good story, and their short chapters make them ideal for reading at bedtime.

Other books by Robert Kingsley Hawes

The Magpie Way
Finding Alice

The Magpie Way
The Great River

A Dog on the Run

When Pop Took Us Fishing

THE GIRL IN THE YELLOW HAT

The Jetty War

Robert Kingsley Hawes

Published by Smile Time

ISBN 978-0-6452189-3-0 (paperback)

First edition, 2023

For book orders and enquiries, contact: r.hawes70@gmail.com

A catalogue record for this book is available from the National Library of Australia

CONTENTS

CONTENTS

1

BACK HOME AGAIN

Being a kid in 1957 was very different to how it is to be a kid today. Back then, only the well-off owned cars and few had ever seen a TV because TV was still two years away for most Australian cities. When at home, kids read books, listened to the wireless, or played board games, which is why most stayed out until dark. They would roam the district on their bikes, looking for things to do. Some of what they did was good, some was bad, but almost all of it was fun. In the town where Jake lived, many of the kids who roamed were new arrivals, their families having immigrated because of the Government's "Populate or Perish" policy. These kids sometimes wandered into places where they were not welcomed, and Jake remembers the time when their rejection gave rise to a conflict they called the jetty war.

It was the summer of 1957 when Jake stepped onto the railway station platform having spent the last three months at boarding school. He had been away from the things he loved, his family, his dog, the seaside, and the fishing. He walked towards the beach, which was how his summer holidays always began, for he would not feel at home until he had once more gazed upon the sea, taken in the salt air, and heard the waves lapping on the sand.

Jake had always seen himself as an outsider, different to the town kids because he spent the best part of each year at boarding school. However, he was also an outsider at the school, because the other kids had rich parents, but his were not rich. He only went there because his grandpa was once the school's principal and had arranged for Jake to be awarded a special scholarship for playing chess.

Jake's friends in his hometown were mainly those who fished with him on the Town Jetty. The town had two jetties, for in many ways, it was two towns. The jetties stood at each end of a bay, one they called the Town Jetty and the other the Old Jetty. The Town Jetty belonged to what most considered to be the true town, where people prospered from the benefits that the post war period had brought.

At the other end of the bay was the Workers Village, made up of settlers' cottages and hastily erected asbestos dwellings, put there to house the ever-increasing number of immigrant families. The true town had shops, nice houses, and a foreshore that boasted of a seaside carnival, whilst the Workers Village just had its beach and the Old Jetty.

'Hey, Jug,' came a voice from the other side of the road.

Jake's nickname was Jug, so called because his full name was Jake Jones, and Jughead Jones was a popular character in the Archie comic books at the time.

'Hi, Gerald, what's new?' Jake replied. Gerald was one of the kids Jake fished with on the Town Jetty.

'The fish are going crazy on the Old Jetty this season,' said Gerald.

Gerald's full name was Gerald Cassidy, so his nickname was Hoppy, after the famous cowboy, Hopalong Cassidy. But no one ever called him Hoppy to his face, for that would be an affront to the Cassidy family, and Hoppy's dad was Councillor Cassidy, the most powerful man in town. Councillor Cassidy was known to take vengeance on anyone who displeased him or his family, simply to prove that he had the power to do it.

Jake wondered about Hoppy's greeting, for it was unusually friendly. He did not like Hoppy, and Hoppy had never been one to offer Jake good fishing advice in the past. However, he thought that Hoppy would be offended if he ignored the tip, and offending a Cassidy was not something a smart person ever did.

Jake arrived at his front gate where he was greeted by a black and white Fox Terrier. The dog leapt into his arms and licked his face.

'Hi, Timmy, I've missed you, fella,' said Jake. He put his favourite animal down and gave him a scruff.

'Woof,' replied the excited dog.

'Been chasing cats again, I see,' said Jake.

Timmy tilted his head.

'Don't give me that innocent look. You have a scratch on your nose. I've warned you, cats fight mean. If you want to bite someone, bite Hoppy.'

'Woof.'

Jake dropped his report card on the ground. 'Grab it, Timmy. Chew it up. Take it away. Bury it somewhere.'

Timmy examined the object with his nose, but that was all. The chance that Jake could tell his parents that the dog had eaten his report card, was gone, but it was a poor plan to begin with. He walked through the back door. 'Hi, Mum, I'm home. Has Timmy been chasing Mrs. Bradly's cat again?'

His mum ignored the question, preferring to give him a firm hug instead.

'Hello, Sweetie, I've missed you so much.'

Jake hugged his mum but felt uncomfortable. Hugging was girls' stuff and being called Sweetie just added to the awkwardness of it all. There had been a time when it would not have bothered him, but it was not for boys who were twelve. Sweetie was also a name for which he was not suited, as his report card would reveal.

His mum asked to see the card in question, which Jake handed over with some reluctance.

'What are the wet marks on the cover?' she asked.

'Timmy wiped his nose on it.'

'How come?'

'I dropped it on the ground.'

'You're lucky he didn't chew it up.'

Jake had his own opinion on that subject but chose not to answer. His mum looked at the school's report. 'How come you got an F for Latin?' she asked.

'I hate the Latin teacher,' said Jake. 'I figured if enough kids got an F, the school might give him the sack.'

'So, how many kids got an F?'

'Only three, I think.'

Jake's plan to get his Latin teacher sacked had gone about as well as his plan to have Timmy eat his report card. But then came the moment he was dreading the most, the special note written by the headmaster.

Jake needs to improve his chess playing skills or he may lose his scholarship. He has also been in several fights this year and if this behaviour persists, the school may be forced to take action.

Jake's report card was proof that he was unworthy of the name Sweetie, but nothing ever seemed fair to him. The rich kids at the school had been teasing him because his parents came from a less privileged background, and he was simply using his fists to prove that kids of lesser privilege still demand respect.

He explained the situation to his mum, and she smiled. 'I know all about it, Sweetie,' she said, 'because the school has been talking to Grandpa. They know the reason you have been fighting and Grandpa is proud of you for sticking up for us, but you must find other ways to settle your differences. Please promise me, that starting from now, you will not resort to using your fists.'

'I will try,' said Jake.

'No. Promise me that you will stop fighting other kids.'

'What if I have to defend myself?'

'Just hold them in a headlock until a responsible adult comes along.'

Jake thought about it. The response to his report card was better than expected, and the headlock idea might work sometimes. 'Okay, I promise,' he said.

Having made a binding commitment to his mum, he headed for his bedroom, dropped his suitcase and kit bag on the floor, and then crashed onto the bed. Everything was as he had left it, apart from being much tidier than when last seen. His mum had done what mums do best, although he failed to notice that she had also washed the curtains, polished the dressing table, and fixed its sticking drawer. He looked at his kit bag, wondering why he had brought schoolbooks home. He had no intention of doing schoolwork for the next seven weeks, and it was with great pleasure that he discarded his school uniform and put on holiday clothes. That marked the official beginning of holiday time, and he had things to do. First on the list was to raid an empty pickle jar from the kitchen. Once found, he shouted to his mum, 'I'm off to Ben's.'

'Okay, Sweetie, dinner will be at six.'

The back door slammed behind him as he left.

Jake had known Ben since the age of three. Ben lived in the house behind and owned a small shop not far from the Town Jetty. He had been the first in the area to own a car, and as a three-year-old, Jake could remember those wonderful mornings when his mum would pass him over the back fence and Ben would take him for a ride around the block.

Jake arrived at Ben's shop which some thought to be a little gloomy, for Ben saw no point in wasting electricity if enough light was coming through the window. But Jake loved Ben's shop, although it was hard to describe what sort of a shop it was. Scattered on its shelves and floor were bicycle parts, hardware, camping gear, fishing gear, and small tins of paint. Ben only stocked the small tins because his customers could not afford the big ones.

However, the item that brought most business to Ben's shop were gents, otherwise known as maggots. These hope-to-be flies were destined to meet an early doom, impaled on a fishhook. Ben received a delivery every day and had a sign in his window that read, *Fresh Gents for Sale*. Some thought his sign was not a good look for the area, and Ben agreed that *fresh* was an odd way to describe a maggot, but the sign remained.

'Hi, Ben, got any gents?' asked Jake.

'It's going to cost you,' smiled his long-time friend.

Ben never charged Jake for gents but gave him jobs instead. It was an arrangement Ben found most beneficial because it gave him cheap labour while stopping Jake from breeding gents at home. Jake had once tried this, and Ben had discovered how unpleasant the smell was when someone bred gents not far from your backdoor.

Jake spent the rest of the afternoon dusting, which was something he would never dream of doing at home. Dusting at home was women's work, but Ben's shop was different. He left the shop with his pickle jar full of gents. That jar was their new home. It was where they would live a life of leisure until chosen to fulfil the purpose for which they were born. Jake regarded gents as having a good life other than for how it was destined to end.

2

AMBUSHED

Jake was up early the next morning because the fish bit best on daylight. He hopped on his bike, leaving a disappointed Timmy at home. Normally, he would have gone to the Town Jetty where he knew everyone, but Hoppy's tip had him curious, so he headed for the Old Jetty instead. The kids who fished there mainly came from the Workers Village, and many had non-English sounding names, but Australia was the only country they had ever known.

Jake propped his bike against the jetty rail, then walked to where some boys were fishing. None noticed as he walked behind them, joining onto the far end of their group. Jake had few claims to fame. He was no good at sport, only average at school, but he could catch fish better than most.

He sat on the jetty rail, which was how most twelve-year-olds fished. Adults could fish over it, but the rail was too high for most kids. Like Jake, they were all sitting on the rail.

Jake checked what the others were doing and thought most to be poor anglers. Their casts were only average, they missed bites, and some were getting tangled. But the kid next to him was the most hopeless of them all. He was using gear that he had probably found in a rubbish bin. The reel was too big, and the rod looked more like a broomstick. Added to this, he was wearing a floppy, yellow hat. *No self-respecting kid would ever wear a hat like that when they were fishing*, thought Jake.

Everyone was fishing for garfish, their floats bobbing in a neat row a short distance out from the jetty. Jake cast his float out to the rest, and soon, people were noticing that he was catching more fish than his share. He sensed their annoyance and began to feel uncomfortable, for he was among strangers, and some were catching nothing at all, including the kid in the yellow hat.

'Would you like to try my fresh gents, mate?' Jake asked his yellow hatted neighbour, hoping that a friendly gesture might ease the tension he was feeling.

The fellow angler did not reply, nor look in Jake's direction.

Jake shrugged and kept fishing, thinking it best to ignore the rude response. Then something unusual happened. It was proof that he was among some of the clumsiest anglers he had ever met. A jar of gents was drifting towards the floats. He stared at the jar. It was almost full. *Shame,* he thought. *How could anyone drop a jar of gents over the side?* Then he noticed a coincidence. The jar was exactly the same as the pickle jar he had borrowed from his mum's kitchen. He looked behind. His jar of gents was gone, then realisation struck. His gents were enjoying an unexpected ocean voyage.

Jake thought that the kid next to him was the obvious culprit, for he had been gone at about the time his gents would have been taken. He glared at the kid and pointed to his gents sailing into the distance.

'Who did that?' he growled.

The kid kept looking away and did not answer.

A surge of anger came over Jake. The kid was obviously guilty and was scared to show his face because he was laughing. He deserved to be pushed off the rail. *Everyone get ready to hear a splash,* he thought, but then he remembered the promise made to his mum. He was to avoid fighting, and besides, the kid might not be able to swim.

Then a voice came from further along the Jetty. 'Don't tell him, Doolittle.'

It appeared that the immigrant kids also had nicknames, and the kid in the yellow hat was called Doolittle.

Jake looked to see who was doing the yelling. It was a kid in a plain, blue t-shirt, with a number six on the back. Jake thought the outfit was best suited for a prisoner on a road gang. *What's your problem, Prisoner Six,* he thought.

But Prisoner Six then chuckled and said to Jake, 'Did you lose your gents, mate?'

Then came another voice. 'Better go home, sonny. You can't catch fish without bait.'

They all began to laugh, and with good reason. Jake's fishing was over for the day. They had won. The only one not laughing was the kid in the yellow hat. He was obviously being cautious because Jake was within striking distance.

What a coward, thought Jake as he stomped towards his bike. Then Prisoner Six stood in front of him.

'We don't want you Town Jetty kids fishing here,' said Prisoner Six. 'This is our jetty, so don't come back, or I will do more than just chuck your gents in next time.'

Prisoner Six was obviously the guilty party, and Jake was tempted to punch him in the nose, but the promise made to his mum stopped him. Also, there was the possibility of bad consequences. He was among friends, but they were not his, and all looked ready for a fight.

Jake walked back to his bike and discovered that his humiliation was not yet over. The tyres were flat, and to make matters worse, the valves had been removed. They had left the pump, but it was useless without the valves. A roar of laughter came from behind, but he did not look back. He walked away, wheeling his bike beside him. His humiliation was complete. He had been defeated, but then footsteps came from behind. Someone was in a hurry, and that person soon overtook him. It was the kid in the yellow hat, and he paused a short distance ahead, putting something on the jetty rail. Then he turned and removed his hat. Blond hair fell to her shoulders, and she smiled. The kid in the yellow hat was a girl.

'You will need these,' she said.

'What?'

'Can't talk to you. They think I'm rushing to the toilet.'

She ran off, leaving Jake standing there, bewildered.

He went to the rail and found two bike valves. She had put them there. They were different to the type taken from his bike but would do the same job. Once out of sight of his tormentors, he popped in the valves, pumped up the tyres, and rode home.

Jake found himself in a strange mood that day, for thoughts of that morning stayed with him. He could not remember the last time anyone had shown him a random act of kindness. He thought about the girl, her hair falling to her shoulders, and her smile. It was not the smile of someone who had won victory over him, for it was neither a smirk nor a sneer. It was simply a smile, a friendly glance. He should have been angry, those kids had humiliated him, but he found himself thinking only about Doolittle. Why had she done that? He knew nothing about girls because he went to an all-boys school. That jetty was boys' territory, but she had invaded their realm and given aid to their enemy.

3

THE JETTY WAR

Ben was surprised when Jake came into the shop for more gents that day. He thought he had given him enough to last the week. 'How come you are back for more?' he asked.

Jake told about the unexpected hostility he had met at the Old Jetty, and about his gents going on an ocean voyage, but he left out the bit about the girl. A girl coming to his aid was something no one needed to know about.

'Why did you go to the Old Jetty?' asked Ben.

'Hoppy said I should.'

'You believed him?'

'Why not?'

'It was Hoppy who started the jetty war.'

'What jetty war?'

Ben told how a kid from the Old Jetty had gone to the Town Jetty and was catching more fish than Hoppy, so Hoppy threw the kid's bike in the water.

'I guess that would have caused a fight,' said Jake.

'No,' said Ben. 'Most kids know that if you hurt Hoppy, the Cassidy family will take revenge.'

'So, the kid just walked away then?'

'Not at first,' said Ben. 'The kid didn't know who Hoppy was, so he went to hit him, but your mate, Boof, stopped him. Boof told the kid that Hoppy was an untouchable, and bad things would happen to anyone who hit him, so the kid declared war instead. He said that any Town Jetty snob who steps foot on the Old Jetty will get beaten up in future.'

'What happened to the bike?' Jake asked.

'The kid retrieved it at low tide.'

'I'm glad to hear that,' Jake replied, 'but that is just the sort of stupid thing Hoppy does because he knows he can get away with it.'

'Yes, it was stupid,' agreed Ben. 'I guess you won't be going to the Old Jetty anymore.'

'Why not?'

'Hoppy didn't just stop at throwing the bike in the water,' said Ben. 'He formed a gang with himself as leader, and he offered free merry-go-round tickets to anyone who joined. When the kids from the other jetty heard about it, they formed their own gang. There is now a jetty war going on and you have just had your first run in with the Old Jetty Gang.'

'But I fish on both jetties,' said Jake, 'and I don't want to join a gang or get free merry-go-round tickets.'

Ben shrugged. 'That doesn't seem to matter,' he said. 'It appears that the Old Jetty kids have branded you a member of Hoppy's gang and I suggest you stay off their jetty in future.

'But how come Hoppy has free merry-go-round tickets?' asked Jake.

'I think his dad is a friend of the owner,' Ben replied, and then he handed Jake a broom and pointed to the floor. 'Your reward for sweeping will be another jar of gents,' he chuckled. 'Best guard them better this time because I am running out of jobs to give you.'

4

THE GIRL IN THE YELLOW HAT

Jake was up before sunrise the next morning. The fish awaited, and normally he would be thinking about the first bite, the hook up, and landing that first fish. It was the most exciting part of the day. The first bite signalled that the fish were there, and a good time was about to be had by all. But Jake's thoughts were elsewhere that morning. He was still thinking about the girl. Why had she bothered to be there so early with gear that was useless for catching garfish. He thought that someone should be helping her, but more importantly, he wondered why she had helped him. Was she on the jetty every morning or had her being there that day been a random thing? He would like to have known more about her, but returning to the Old Jetty was not an option.

Jake had a morning routine that never changed because he was always too sleepy to do otherwise, but this morning became the exception. He went searching for a pair of fold-up opera glasses given to him by his grandpa. Once found, he put them in his pocket, then set out for the Town Jetty. He took up his usual spot beside his best mate, Boof, so named because his favourite comic character was Boof Head. The garfish they were after, schooled over a small area, causing the kids to fish in a tight group, and all were eager to catch the first fish. Catching the first fish brought almost the same bragging rights as catching the most, and Jake was always keen to be the one who caught the first, but on this day, he was slow off the mark. Boof noticed him standing there, staring towards the Old Jetty. 'What are you looking at?' he asked.

'Nothing.'

Jake had not answered truthfully, but he could hardly tell Boof that he was looking for a girl in a yellow hat. He could see the Old Jetty kids gathered in a group, but at that distance, they were just a dark blob stretched along part of the Old Jetty. He had hoped to see a dot of

13

yellow in the midst of that blob, but the light was poor. He took out his opera glasses.

'You must be looking at something,' said Boof.

'No. Just testing my opera glasses. Seeing if they work.'

'Well, do they? Can I have a look?'

'No.'

The sun had not long appeared, its first rays barely breaking through the broken cloud, and the opera glasses could reveal nothing in the poor light.

Jake stopped looking, hoping that Boof would ask no more questions, and a fish saved the day. Boof got the first bite, and he landed the first fish. Bragging rights were his, and Jake had yet to put his line in the water.

'You are a bit slow today,' laughed Boof.

'I bet I still catch more than you,' was Jake's reply.

'Okay, the competition is on.'

Catching garfish was an art that required mindless concentration, which was one of Jake's strengths. To be successful, the angler had to fix his eyes on the float, wait for its slightest move, then time the strike to the fraction of a second. Catching garfish was something Jake had mastered, and he was confident that he could beat his friend.

The light got better, causing Jake to keep looking at the Old Jetty, but he saw nothing yellow.

'You just missed a bite,' laughed Boof, who now had three fish in the bag.

Darn, thought Jake. He pulled in his float and discovered that the fish had stripped his hooks almost bare, proof that he had not been concentrating.

Boof pulled in another fish, but Jake hardly noticed. He was kneeling beside his tackle box, putting on more bait, but his thoughts were elsewhere. He was wondering if she was fishing, and if so, what she had caught? Then he wondered how she could ever catch a fish with a rod that more closely resembled a broomstick.

A beam of light broke through the cloud, striking the Old Jetty. It fell on the kids fishing there, and Jake thought he caught a glimpse of yellow, but the light moved on. Had he imagined it, or could he really see her hat from that distance? He wanted to take out his opera glasses, but that would only make Boof curious.

Sometime later, the fish started going off the bite, and Boof was ahead on catch. 'Hey guys,' he shouted, 'I finally beat Jug, and I caught the first fish as well.'

It was Boof's best result ever, and he was enjoying the moment, but Jake was off his game. His heart had not been in the contest, for he had been too busy looking elsewhere rather than at his float.

The sun rose higher, and it was time for the fish to leave the shallows. The kids began packing up, and Jake knew that the same would be happening on the Old Jetty. He looked towards it once more. The Old Jetty kids were still there, but not for much longer, and he was yet to confirm if one of them was wearing a yellow hat. He needed to use his opera glasses but did not want Boof asking more questions. He waited, hoping for Boof to leave, but Boof stayed on. Boof was enjoying his moment of victory, leaving Jake with no choice. He brought out the glasses again, hoping to have a sneak look while Boof was busy bragging, but everything was blurred. *Darn,* he thought. He adjusted the focus and looked again. This time he saw a patch of colour, but it was red. He was looking at the jetty's lifebuoy, so he turned his attention closer to shore. There he saw the kids, and some were leaving, and he thought that some might have already left. He also thought that the girl might be wearing a different coloured hat. Then suddenly, there it was. A tiny dot of yellow on the edge of the main group, in the exact same spot that he had seen the girl the day before. *She must go every day,* he thought.

However, so distracted had Jake been by his focusing problems, that he had forgotten about Boof who was now staring at him. 'What are you looking at?' asked his friend.

'Er, it's a secret,' said Jake, suddenly realising his mistake.

'Tell me.'

'No.'

'Let me look through your opera glasses.'

Jake upset the focus and handed them over. 'Okay, here they are. What can you see?'

'Nothing, your opera glasses don't work.'

Boof handed them back, thinking that boarding school was turning Jug into a rather strange person.

5

A VISIT TO THE DUMP

Jake never let a holiday go by without making at least one trip to the dump. It was a place that was popular with most kids, and some went there every day. The regulars were known as the Dump Kids.

The dump was a place Jake would visit on days that were too windy to go fishing, and the day that followed was such a day. He headed for the dump, but wind is not the friend of someone who travels by bike. Tailwinds were great because record-breaking speeds could be reached, but a slog into a head wind was the price you had to pay when forced to go back the other way.

Jake timed his arrival that day to coincide with a special event, the daily visit of the car factory truck. Most things found at the dump were old, but not everything. The things that came on that truck were all new. Hidden among the scraps from the workers' canteen would be rear vision mirrors, car fittings, and vinyl offcuts from the interior trim section.

The truck arrived right on time and the Dump Kids watched it, as did Jake, and as did the ever-present flock of seagulls. Everyone wanted to know where the load would be dumped, for most treasures were found by the first scavengers to pick it over. The driver chose a spot some distance away which signalled the start of the Daily Dump Dash. All were keen to get there first, and Jake was in the lead, but he stopped when something caught his eye. The other kids ran past him.

Lying on the ground was something Jake found hard to believe. It was a bike, and he knew the owner. It was Hoppy's bike, but how could that be? Hoppy's bike was the envy of all the kids. It was new, had chrome rims, and a lighting set powered by a generator. Jake took a closer look. It was Hoppy's bike for sure. No other kid in the town had a bike anywhere near as good as Hoppy's.

However, Hoppy's bike was now a wreck, completely crushed in places. Even King Kong, the monster gorilla that terrorised audiences at the pictures, was not capable of such destruction. Jake stared at the bike, but then another thought struck him. Was Hoppy riding it at the time?' He looked closer. No blood. He turned it over. No blood on the other side either. That was a good sign. Jake did not like Hoppy, but he still hoped that no harm had come to him.

Then Jake had a brain wave. He owed two bike valves to the girl in the yellow hat. He had even thought of doing jobs for Ben in exchange for a pair, but Ben was running out of jobs to give. However, Hoppy's bike had two valves and they were almost new. But then conscience kicked in. What if Hoppy was dead? Taking those valves would be like stealing the belongings from the body of a dead soldier. Hoppy could be looking down from heaven right now.

Jake stood there thinking. There was no blood. The chances were that Hoppy was still alive. To leave the valves there for someone else to take would be stupid. Then there was always the option of bringing them back if the worst had happened. He took the valves.

Jake arrived at Ben's shop not long before closing time, and Ben told him the sad tale. Hoppy had gone to his father's hardware store, parking his bike under the shop's front veranda. Sometime later, he had headed for home, but disaster struck when he reached the train crossing. The bike jolted as it crossed the rails, causing the bike's generator to shake loose and slide down the front fork.

The generator was an essential part of a bike's lighting set in 1957. It was clamped to the front fork and had a driving knob that could be pressed against the tyre. It powered the lights, but only while the bike was moving. It also had another problem. If the generator came loose, it could slide down the fork and into the spokes, causing the bike to come to a sudden and violent halt. Somehow, that is what had happened to Hoppy's bike, and he had gone flying over the handlebars, face first onto the railway tracks.

Ben continued the story but was finding it hard not to laugh, because he considered Hoppy and his dad to be his enemies. Councillor Cassidy had been trying to put Ben out of business because both owned hardware stores, but it was a mean-spirited thing to do, because Councillor Cassidy had many business interests whilst Ben only had his little shop. In recent times, someone had begun a campaign for Ben's shop to be closed, with people being told that the annual influx of summer flies was due to his maggot selling enterprise. Hoppy had even been seen putting pamphlets in letter boxes, proof that his father was behind the campaign.

Jake waited for Ben to regain composure, then heard him describe how Hoppy had laid on the rails, pretending to be unconscious, hoping for sympathy from a lady who had seen him fall. But when the lady ran to his aid, she saw blood on his face, and the sight of blood sent her into a tizz, so Hoppy began to cry, neither noticing that the crossing bells had begun to ring. Then the lady looked up, saw the train coming, so she panicked and dragged Hoppy off the rails, but there was no real danger. The train was on the other track, but unfortunately, so was Hoppy's bike.

When Hoppy sat up, he saw the train coming, smoke streaming from its smokestack. Then he realised the worst. His bike was about to be run down and it was all too late, the train was not slowing down. The bike was doomed, its final destruction barely audible above the sound of clattering wheels, but Hoppy did hear the train driver shout, 'Sorry.'

Jake thought that the sad demise of Hoppy's bike would be an incident soon forgotten, but then Ben told him that would not be the case. Hoppy's dad had fitted the generator himself and was convinced that sabotage was involved. The fixing screws could never have come loose of their own accord. Someone had loosened them, a suspicion he shared with Officer Biggs, the local policeman. He said that Ben had probably paid Jake to do the foul deed because Ben had heard a rumour that Hoppy had distributed nasty pamphlets about his shop.

Then Ben told how the incident was now the subject of a police investigation, with him and Jake as the main suspects. From now on, they would be under the watchful eye of the law. It was Councillor

Cassidy's opinion, that someone had committed an act of attempted murder on his son, as his son could have been killed by the train. He had even put a reward poster in his shop window to assist with the investigation.

6

A BAD PLAN

Jake was not one who gave up easily, and for a reason he could not explain, he needed to know more about the girl in the yellow hat. He had known very few girls, and the ones he did, were boring. They played with dolls, liked dressing up, and were into dancing and stuff. He also felt that girls did not like him, not that it mattered. But the girl in the yellow hat was different. She liked fishing, mixed with the tough kids, and had been kind to him. At the very least, he needed to return her bike valves. But returning the valves meant going to the Old Jetty, and the risks were obvious. His stay there would have to be short, perhaps even violent, but he could think of no other way of reaching her.

Venturing into enemy territory was a situation that called for backup, but the Town Jetty kids were not an option. None of them would risk a brawl just to speak to a girl, which left Jake with only one choice. He had to call on Timmy, and Timmy was up for the job, although he did not know what the job was when he volunteered for it. He only knew that he would be going somewhere with Jake, and any excuse to escape the yard was good for him.

Next morning, the duo set off for the Old Jetty, Jake on his bike and Timmy running behind. They travelled along the esplanade, passing the houses of the wealthy. Then they paused at the warning seat, so named because of a sign that stood next to it. The sign read *Beware of Sharks* and had been placed there following a suspected shark attack. It marked the last place a boy was seen prior to setting out in his canoe. Only the canoe came back, washed up in the late afternoon, a huge hole bitten in its hull.

The warning seat sat midway between the two jetties and marked the beginning of the Workers Village. Once past it, Jake would be in enemy territory and could come across hostile kids. He pulled out his opera glasses, hoping to see a yellow hat in the early morning light, and he did. She was there, on the Old Jetty, but she would not be easy to reach. He would have to sneak past the other kids to get to her.

He arrived at the jetty and propped his bike against the jetty rail, making sure it was above sand and not water. That way, he would not have to wait until low tide should someone throw it over the side. It was also well placed for a quick getaway. Once having laid out his method of escape, his next move was to sneak past the kids while they were watching their floats. 'Wait here and guard the bike,' he said to Timmy, but Timmy was a dog of action, and sitting next to Jake's bike held no appeal. He sniffed the air and detected something of interest, something that a dog like him might like to eat.

The kids were using burley, which they squeezed into their floats to attract fish. It was made from chook food, and each kid had a small tub of it sitting beside them. Unfortunately, Timmy had left home without breakfast that morning, and he was not a fussy eater. Anything good enough for the chooks, was good enough for him.

Jake was within a short distance of reaching the girl when someone yelled, 'Who owns this stupid dog?' Timmy had his snout in Prisoner Six's burley tub. The kids all turned around.

'Sorry,' said Jake. 'I was just taking my dog for a walk, and he decided to run up the jetty.'

'You're the Town Jetty kid we threw off here a couple of days ago,' said Prisoner Six.

'You only did that to my gents,' said Jake. 'I left of my own accord.'

The kids stopped fishing and Jake was surrounded. Only the girl in the yellow hat remained where she was. She was sitting on the jetty rail, signalling for Jake to run, but it was too late for that.

A kid yelled out, 'I've got his bike. What shall I do with it?'

Jake turned. A kid was on his bike, doing skids on the jetty. 'Get him, Timmy,' Jake shouted, but Timmy had a better idea. There was a seagull resting not far away, and Timmy saw it as his canine duty to send that annoying bird on its way.

Prisoner Six grabbed a handful of burley. 'How would you like this squashed in your hair?' he said, but then came a voice.

'Don't be stupid, Ivan. You know the rules.'

It was the girl in the yellow hat. Ivan gave her a brief glance, then held the handful of burley to Jake's face. 'You are lucky this time, but this is your last warning,' he said. 'Stay off our jetty.'

The girl in the yellow hat shouted again. 'Give him back his bike and let him go.'

The kids did as she asked and Jake was soon on his way, but the mystery of the girl was now deeper than ever. Was she the leader of the Old Jetty Gang, and if so, why would a tough gang of boys choose a girl to be their leader?

Timmy followed Jake home, feeling pleased with his morning's work. He had shown that seagull that he was the boss. Dogs ruled, they owned the jetty, and seagulls could but fly away. However, he was unaware that his reputation as a guard dog was no more. Once home, Jake frowned at his black and white companion.

'You have failed in your duty,' he growled.

'Woof.'

'Don't woof me and stop wagging your tail.'

'Woof.'

'That's it. I hereby give you a dishonourable discharge. You may no longer call yourself a guard dog.'

'Woof.'

Jake shook his head. Lecturing Timmy was a waste of time. It was as if he never understood a word being said.

7

HOW TO IMPRESS A GIRL

The following day was a Sunday, and Jake regarded Sundays as the only blemish on his otherwise perfect summer holiday. He would have to go to Sunday School, which was unfair because none of his friends went, and his parents never went to church. What is good for the goose should be good for the gander, Jake reckoned, but it was not so in his case. He was a goose whose freedom was being denied on a Sunday, while the ganders were at home doing whatever they liked.

Jake had been going to Sunday School for years and his opinion of the place had never changed. For him, Sunday School itself was not the problem, it was just that it was always held on a Sunday. He believed that it should be held on a weekday, because weekends and school holidays should be left for kids to do whatever they liked. Also, like college, Sunday School was another place where he felt an outsider. He was the only kid whose parents never went to the church, and he blamed that as the reason he had never won a prize at a Sunday School picnic.

He put on his best clothes that morning, for Sunday School required him to be neatly dressed, which was yet another reason for him not to like the place. But his mum thought he looked splendid, dressed in his best shorts, white shirt, long socks, and a ridiculous brimmed hat. She gave him an envelope as he was leaving. 'Give this to Miss Brown,' she said. 'In it is a photo taken at the Sunday School's first picnic. I told her you would be bringing it today.'

Jake underwent a final inspection, this time his mum saying, 'You are leaving a bit early, Sweetie, but being early is a nice habit to get into.'

Jake agreed and was out the door, but he had no intention of being early for Sunday School. He headed for the warning seat, from where he could check out the Old Jetty. He thought that if the girl in the yellow hat went home early, he might be able to follow her and see where she lived.

He arrived at the warning seat where he found Bottles, the man of mystery who often sat on that seat. Bottles had been around for as long as Jake could remember, and most thought him to be slow-witted, but Jake knew better. Everyone knew Bottles, for they would see him dragging his cart around town, collecting bottles, but no one knew much more about him than that.

No one had ever seen his face because it was always covered by a large handkerchief. Had he lived in the days of the wild west, the sheriff would have shot him, thinking he was about to rob the bank. Added to this, Bottles never spoke, although he could mumble a few words if necessary, but mostly he just said, 'Ug.'

Jake gave Bottles his usual greeting. 'Ug, Bottles, how are you today?'

'Ug,' Bottles replied, along with a thumbs up. Jake had always felt that Bottles and he had a special relationship, because ug and jug sounded almost the same. It was as if Jake was the only person Bottles could call by name.

Bottles pointed towards the end of the Old Jetty. 'Ug,' he said, so Jake pulled out his opera glasses but saw nothing of interest. The kids were fishing in the shallows but there was no one at the end of the jetty. He stopped looking, but Bottles shook his head. 'Ug,' he repeated, this time sounding a bit more forceful. Then he pointed again.

Jake looked through the opera glasses once more. 'There is no one on the end of the jetty,' he said.

Bottles motioned his arm, as if it were a swimming fish.

Jake looked again, and this time he saw them. The water around the end of the jetty was black with salmon. The school was packed tight, possibly taking shelter from a shark. His heart began to race, and then it sank. Had it not been a Sunday, and had there not been a jetty war, those salmon would give him the fishing experience of a lifetime, but it was just not possible.

He thought about telling the Old Jetty kids about the opportunity that awaited at the end of the jetty, and they might bury the hatchet, but what would be the point? None of them had the gear necessary. It would take a rod built like a broomstick to handle those big fish.

Then it came to him, a plan so bold that it would probably not work, but it was worth a try. Those salmon were unlikely to ever return, and this might be his best chance to impress the girl in the yellow hat. He could see her with his opera glasses, and as always, she was on the seaward side of the group. He hopped on his bike and raced at full speed, along the esplanade and then up the jetty. He zoomed past the kids who were fishing, but none bothered to turn around. A couple had seen him coming, but no one expected a member of the Town Jetty Gang to be wearing Sunday School clothes.

Jake pulled up beside the girl, and she turned around. *It's the kid from the Town Jetty,* she thought. *Why is he back? Does he have a death wish or something, and why is he all dressed up?'* She gave him a polite, 'Hello.'

Jake skipped the formalities. 'Meet me at the end of the jetty,' he said. 'Bring your fishing gear and don't tell the others.' He rode off, not knowing if he had just made a fool of himself, or whether she would do what he had said.

The girl was curious. This was the third day the Town Jetty kid had been there, and she wondered if it was to see her, but she quickly dismissed that idea. But he was nicely dressed, which was certainly a good way to make an impression on a girl. She picked up her fishing gear and joined him.

'Hi, I'm Jake,' said Jake.

'Hello, Jake, I'm Eliza. Why am I here?'

'Look.' He pointed to the water.

'Are they fish?' gasped Eliza. She could not believe her eyes.

'Yes, they are salmon. I have been fishing all my life but have never seen them here like this before.'

They gazed in awe at the massive school. The fish were docile, a mosaic of blue bodies packed close together, just below the surface.

On occasions, one would show a flash of silver as it jostled to hold position in the school.

'They are huge. Do you think I could catch one?' asked Eliza.

'That's the plan. Have you got any big hooks?'

Eliza reached into her tackle box. 'Is this one big enough?'

'That's perfect,' said Jake, 'What have you been using a hook like that for?'

'I have never used it,' she said. 'I found it on the jetty the other day and it was shiny and new, so I picked it up.'

'Have you got a fish we could use for bait?' asked Jake.

'No.'

'Surely you have caught at least one fish this morning?'

'Don't be rude. I am only a learner.'

'Sorry,' said Jake. 'We will just have to try with a bare hook.'

'I thought fish only took a hook if it had bait on it,' Eliza queried.

'Hungry salmon will sometimes grab anything shiny,' said Jake. 'Drop the hook through the school and see what happens.'

Eliza hopped onto the jetty rail causing Jake to issue a warning. 'Make sure you keep a firm grip on the rod and don't lean forward, or the fish will pull you in,' he said.

She lowered the hook into the water.

Now give the hook a jiggle, thought Jake, but he had no time to say it, because it was already in the mouth of a hungry salmon. The startled fish powered towards open water, causing Eliza to discover the reason for Jake's warning. He put his arm around her waist to stop her going over the side.

Eliza leant back and regained her balance. 'I'm okay now, I think.'

Jake released his grip and watched. 'Take it easy,' he said. 'Let the fish tire himself. Don't try to land him until he is exhausted.'

'Wow, Wow, Wow!' exclaimed Eliza. 'This is so exciting.'

The fish swam in an arc and then began to leap out of the water, each leap causing another exclamation of, 'Wow!'

'Salmon are the most exciting fish you can catch,' said Jake. 'They always leap like that.'

'They are fantastic!' said the excited fisher-girl.

A tense struggle followed, but to no avail for the salmon. The exhausted fish was finally swimming lazily on the surface. 'I can't lift it,' said Eliza. 'It's too heavy.'

Eliza was right. Even her broomstick rod was not strong enough to lift a three-pound salmon. Jake would have to go down and retrieve it by hand. 'Ease it close to that ladder,' he said.

'Okay.'

Then he asked, 'Do you have a landing net?'

'How could I fit a landing net in my tackle box?'

'Good question,' Jake shrugged. 'I guess you don't have a gaff either?'

'What's a gaff?'

'Don't worry, I will think of something.'

Jake climbed down the ladder, but he had no idea how to grab a swimming fish. Then, in what seemed like a flash, the school was gone. *Have I just spooked 50-ton of salmon?* he thought, but then another thought came to him. *Perhaps a shark is after them.* 'Can you see a shark anywhere?' he shouted.

'No.'

'Not even under the jetty?'

'I can't see under the jetty.'

To catch a fish with your bare hands while watching out for a shark was a difficult thing for someone to do while dressed for Sunday School. A normal person would have given up, but Jake was determined to catch that fish because he wanted to impress Eliza.

He climbed to the bottom rung and grabbed the line, easing the exhausted fish to within an arm's length. 'Lift its head out of the water,' he shouted, which Eliza did.

Jake reached down and grabbed the fish by the head, sinking his fingers into its gills. It was the most difficult part of the job, and it had gone off without a hitch, but things did not go so well after that. His foot was on the bottom rung and the next wave filled his shoe. Then the fish gave a kick, so Jake pressed it firm against his chest, successfully foiling the attempted escape, but he now had blood and slime on his shirt.

He climbed up the ladder and dropped the fish onto the jetty. Then he inspected the unfortunate state of his clothes, but Eliza only had eyes for the fish. *Did I just catch that?* she thought. *Did I really catch that? The boys are going to be so annoyed when they see what I have caught.*

But Jake could only think about the trouble he was in. He had to go to Sunday School because he had a photo to give Miss Brown. He looked at his watch and discovered that he was now running late, something else that he would be in trouble for. 'I have to go,' he said. 'Do you know Ben's Hardware Store?'

'Everyone knows Ben's Hardware.'

'Good,' said Jake. 'I have bike valves to return to you. Perhaps I might see you there tomorrow afternoon.'

'Okay,' said Eliza. still looking in amazement at the fish that lay at her feet.

Jake hurried away, racing past the kids without incident, and only Bottles saw him as he hurtled past the warning seat. Bottles saw the salmon blood on Jake's shirt and gave a thumbs up, but Jake was in no mood to celebrate his proof of victory.

8

TROUBLE IN SUNDAY SCHOOL

As expected, Jake arrived late for Sunday School. He opened the door and walked in, gasping for breath after his fast ride. The kids were all sitting down, paying close attention to Miss Brown who was reading. Silence fell upon the room as Jake entered.

'You're late,' said Miss Brown.

Jake heard several muffled giggles. 'Sorry, Miss. I had a small accident getting here.' He walked to the back of the class, but it was not a silent walk. His shoe was still half full of water. Squelch, clomp, squelch, clomp. It was as if he had a small washing machine attached to his leg. Jake sat down, but now everyone was giggling.

'Did you step in a puddle?' asked Miss Brown.

Jake waited for the giggles to subside then answered, 'Yes, Miss, a very big one.'

Then Miss Brown remembered the photo. 'Oh, Jake. Your mother said that you were bringing a photo of the Sunday School's first picnic. She said we both went to it. I would like to pass it around the room.'

So, Mum was made to come here when she was a girl, thought Jake. *Now I know why she is taking it out on me.* But Jake had a problem. His shirt had salmon blood on it. To date, he had hidden the splodge by holding his hat to his chest. No one thought it unusual because he was out of breath, but he could not keep doing it.

He squelched to the front, still holding his chest. 'Are you having a heart attack?' giggled Susie as he squelched by.

'Maybe,' said Jake. He reached into his shirt pocket and pulled out the envelope, but to his horror, it had blood on it. Jake stood frozen, one hand holding the hat to his chest, the other holding a blood-stained envelope.

'Can I have the envelope please,' said Miss Brown.

'Let me take the photo out of it for you,' said Jake, but he found it difficult to open the envelope while still holding the hat to his chest.

'You look silly,' giggled Susie. 'Why don't you put your hat down?'

'Quiet, Susie,' said Miss Brown, and then she said to Jake in a much firmer voice, 'Give me the envelope, please.'

Jake did as he was told, knowing that his problems were about to get worse. 'Jake, that looks like blood on this envelope,' gasped Miss Brown.

'Er, yes, I think it is.'

'Yuck, why are you giving it to me?'

'Because you asked for it.'

'But why are you holding your hat like that?'

Jake had to show all, for to do otherwise would require him to make up a fanciful story, and lying was not an option. He was on church premises and a lie told within those walls could have eternal consequences. He revealed his blood-stained shirt. 'It's alright. It's not my blood,' he said.

Miss Brown was horrified. She turned away because she hated the sight of blood. Susie put up her hand. 'I bet Jake gave some kid a blood-nose,' she said.

'That is too much blood for a blood-nose,' reasoned Miss Brown.

'But some kids have really big noses,' Susie giggled. 'Jake might have hit one of them.'

Poor Miss Brown. Her training had not prepared her for something like this. What to do when a kid turns up covered in blood was a subject not covered in the Sunday School Teacher's Manual. 'Jake, you are causing a disruption,' she said. 'Go to the back of the class. We will talk about this later.'

Jake squelched his way to the back, which was where kids were told to sit if Miss Brown was displeased with them, but it was not long before Susie had her hand up again.

'Miss Brown, I can smell something fishy.'

'So can I,' said another girl.

'Now you mention it, Jake's envelope smells a bit that way,' said Miss Brown. 'Jake, can you tell us anything about an unpleasant smell of fish in the room?'

'No,' said Jake, and he felt that he had spoken truthfully. He was a true angler, and no true angler ever regarded fish as smelling unpleasant.

Miss Brown walked to the back of the class and stood next to him, then took a deep breath. 'Jake, the smell is coming from you.'

'I knew it was Jake,' said Susie.

Miss Brown pointed to the far corner of the room. 'Go and sit over there where the others can't smell you,' she said. 'We will talk about this when everyone else has gone home.' Then she handed back the envelope, which she had not opened due to its distasteful condition.

Jake spent the rest of the lesson in the naughty corner, then once the others had left, Miss Brown gave him the promised lecture. 'Jake,' she said. 'Your mother is worried that the only kids you have anything to do with are the ones you know at the jetty, so she sends you here to meet some nicer children, but you seem to have trouble fitting in. It might be for the better if you don't come again. I will talk it over with your mother.'

Jake left Sunday School with mixed feelings. His days of going there might be over. That would be a good thing, but then he thought about his mum. She would become known as the only mum in town to ever have a kid expelled from Sunday School. That would be bad.

He went to the beach and sat on the warning seat, the place where Bottles often sat. *This is probably the place where outsiders are meant to be,* he thought, but then a different thought came to him. He was not an outsider like Bottles. He was just a kid that not everyone liked, but he could do nothing about how they felt. They just added value to the people who were his friends. Bottles was the only person who had a problem, and Jake was beginning to understand the world from Bottles' viewpoint.

He went home and explained the unfortunate state of his clothes to his mum, and how he had been caught up in a once in a lifetime event.

He told how he had helped someone catch a salmon, but he gave no details on who he had helped. The girl in the yellow hat was someone he wanted to keep private.

Then his mum asked if Miss Brown liked the photo, which was another awkward thing that had to be explained. He told how Miss Brown hated the sight of blood, had no appreciation for the smell of fish, and had not seen the photo. He thought he had argued his case well, and he would be seen as the innocent victim in all that had happened, but not so. 'You are grounded for twenty-four hours,' said his mum.

Jake looked at the clock. His sentence would end at precisely 12.25 p.m. the next day. That meant he could be at Ben's shop by 12.30 p.m. if he hurried. He had told Eliza that he would see her there, but she may have come and gone by then.

But that was not the end of his mum's bad news, for she told him that Officer Biggs had called to see her that morning. It appeared that Jake was the main suspect for the sabotage done to Hoppy's bike, and the officer wanted to know where Jake was at the time of the crime.

'What did you tell him?' Jake asked.

'I told him you were home with me.'

'But that was the day I went to the dump,' said Jake.

'Maybe,' said his mum, 'but it doesn't matter. All I know is that you wouldn't do something as silly as that.'

These are the moments when kids realise that their mums are great. Not long before, Jake was conflicted when faced with the possibility of having to tell a lie on church premises, but his mum had no such problem telling a fib to the law. She was doing whatever she thought was necessary to protect her son.

9

A DAY TO FORGET

Jake was someone who always made the best of a bad situation, and for once, he did not have to be out of bed before daylight. He could sleep in, or so he thought. His mum walked into his bedroom much earlier than expected. 'Out of bed,' she said. 'I want to wash your sheets.'

Poor Jake, his day was off to a bad start. The morning sun beamed through the window, telling him that the weather outside was perfect. The kids would all be down the jetty ripping them in, but he still had five hours and twenty-five minutes of his sentence to go. His mood sank and he began to worry what else might go wrong that day. Perhaps Eliza would go to Ben's shop early and then leave, or perhaps she would not go there at all. Then he thought about what would happen once he gave her the bike valves. What excuse could he use to see her again.

Jake always thought that the best thing to do when in a bad mood, was to eat, and his breakfast that morning could have fed the whole family. Then he remembered his old fishing gear in the shed. Perhaps he could give it to Eliza, provided that his mum had not thrown it out.

He raced out and searched, and for the first time that day, something went right. He found his old rod and reel. They were a bit the worse for wear, but he could fix all that. He cleaned and oiled the reel, then varnished the cane rod, giving everything more attention than they had ever been given before. They had to be as good as new, for they were to be a gift for Eliza, his excuse to see her again.

He finished the job just in time for lunch, which meant his grounding was almost over, but then came the next setback for the day. His mum was running late.

'What's for lunch?' he called as he walked through the back door.

'Boiled eggs,' came a voice from somewhere inside the house.

'Where are they?'

'I haven't boiled them yet. I am still dusting the rooms.'

Jake looked at the clock. It was 12.00 p.m. That was when they always had lunch. His mum was not sticking to the schedule.

'Mum, we always have lunch at twelve,' said Jake.

'No, we don't. Sometimes we have it later.'

'We do?'

'Yes, Sweetie, we do. How come this is the first time you have ever worried about what time we have lunch?'

Jake ignored the question. 'What if I help you get it?' he asked. 'Could we have it now?'

'Why?'

'I'm hungry.'

'Sweetie, you had a huge breakfast this morning. How could you possibly be hungry?'

'I am a growing boy. Let me help you with lunch.'

'You are offering to help get lunch?' laughed his mum.

'Yes.'

'That's a first for this house,' she said. 'Your dad has never made that offer. You can start by boiling the eggs.'

'How do I do that?' Jake asked.

'First, you boil the water.'

'In the kettle?'

'No. In a saucepan.'

Jake filled a large saucepan and put it on the stove. 'How do I turn the stove on?' he asked.

'Put the saucepan on the biggest element and then turn the top knob,' said his mum.

'What's an element?'

'The thing that heats the saucepan.'

At that moment, the phone rang. It was Miss Brown, but Jake had already confessed to his crimes and his sentence was almost over. However, Miss Brown's phone calls were never brief. Minutes went by. The clock ticked past 12.25 p.m. Jake's grounding was officially over, but his mum was still on the phone. Twenty more minutes passed before his mum hung up. 'Good news,' she said. 'Miss Brown says you are still welcome to attend Sunday School.'

Blast, thought Jake. Nothing was going right for him that day.

Jake's mum walked into the kitchen. 'What are you doing?' she asked.

'Boiling the water.'

'Sweetie, that is far too much water and you should have the knob turned to high. The water isn't even warm. Get me a smaller saucepan from the cupboard.'

In the years that followed, Jake's cooking skills were to improve, but he was never allowed to forget how he had failed in his first attempt to boil water.

Another thirty minutes passed before Jake finally raced into Ben's shop. 'Hi, Ben, got any jobs for me?' he asked.

'Do you need more gents?'

'No.'

'Then why are you offering to do jobs?'

'I am just being nice.'

Ben shrugged. 'Okay, you can sweep out the shop.'

Jake swept the floor at a leisurely pace, but Eliza did not appear. Finally, Ben said, 'I think you can stop sweeping now or you will wear out the broom.'

'Got any more jobs?' Jake asked.

'Really?' queried Ben, amused by Jake's sudden work ethic.

'Yep, what else can I do?'

'Okay. You can wash the front window.'

Jake dragged the ladder out to the footpath, along with a bucket and sponge. He washed the window and then went back inside. 'Is that clean enough, Ben, or should I wash it some more?'

'That looks good,' Ben replied, and then he said, 'Oh, by the way, a girl came in here looking for you today. She was a real chatterbox and couldn't stop talking about a salmon she caught. She left just before you came in but said she would come back tomorrow.'

Jake was having a day to forget. He had missed a good morning's fishing, done jobs for Ben for no good reason, and his mum had laughed at him because he could not boil water. But at least the girl was coming back tomorrow, he just needed more reasons to be in Ben's shop when she did.

'I have to go now,' said Jake, 'but I will see you tomorrow.'

Jake rushed out of the shop, but stopped when Ben shouted, 'Hey, Jake, come back. The ladder is still on the footpath.'

Jake put the ladder away, but just as he went to leave for a second time, Ben said, 'Don't bother about doing jobs tomorrow. Just come at three. That is when she said she would be here.'

Jake noticed that Ben was smiling as he said it.

10

A DAY TO REMEMBER

The following morning saw Jake back to his normal routine. He was up before sunrise and off to the jetty, for he never wasted time having breakfast when there were fish to be caught.

'Where were you yesterday?' Boof asked him upon arrival.

'I was grounded.'

'Why?'

'I got chucked out of Sunday School.'

'Wow,' said Boof. 'That's fantastic. You must have done something really awful. Tell us about it.'

'I upset the teacher.'

'You upset that nice Miss Brown. What did you do?'

'Nothing. It's not my fault that she doesn't like the sight of blood.'

'I heard she doesn't like the smell of fish either,' laughed Boof.

It appeared that everyone already knew about Jake's problem at Sunday School, but he soon discovered that more details had been added.

'Susie told Hoppy that you were covered in blood,' said Boof.

'No. It was just on my shirt.'

'But what about the smelly squid head you dropped on Susie's lap?'

'That never happened.'

'Pity,' said Boof. 'That was the part of the story I liked the best.'

Jake was having his five minutes of fame, for he was the first kid to ever be chucked out of Sunday School, but he was not prepared for Boof's next question. 'Whose blood was on your shirt?' he asked.

Jake knew that if he said it was salmon blood, the kids would want to know more, which would be a problem. He could hardly tell them that he had been to the Old Jetty and helped a member of the enemy gang catch a salmon, because that would get him banned from fishing off the Town Jetty. 'I can't tell you,' he said, but then Hoppy interrupted.

'I have heard that someone has been going around stabbing people and that Officer Biggs has put you on a watch list.'

'It wasn't even Human blood,' said Jake.

'Then why the big secrecy?'

'Okay, if you must know, it was salmon blood. I helped someone catch a salmon, but the fisherman's code of secrecy prevents me from telling you more.'

The fishermen's code of secrecy was something they all respected, and no more questions were asked, but Hoppy had sown doubts about Jake's character.'

A short while later, Jake said to Boof, 'I don't think anyone believes Hoppy. I think he made up that stabbing story.'

'I am not so sure,' his friend replied. 'I would be careful how you wave your knife about next time you take it out of your tackle box. Some of them are still looking at you in an odd way.'

Jake was surprised that kids he thought to be his friends, would be looking at him with distrust, but he blamed Hoppy for that. He was more concerned about his meeting with Eliza that afternoon, because he wanted to make a good impression on her. What had happened with the kids that morning just increased his feeling of always being an outsider.

He arrived at Ben's shop shortly before the appointed hour of three, but Eliza was already there. She had changed from her fishing clothes into white shorts and a yellow top, but she was still wearing her yellow hat. Jake thought that her top might be new because it still had the price tag hanging from it.

'Hi, Jake,' said Ben. 'Eliza here has been telling me how you helped her catch a salmon.'

'Oh,' said Jake.

'Yes, and I have been telling her all about you.'

'Like what?'

'Nothing special. You can ask her yourself later.'

Jake felt awkward and was not sure what to say. She had come dressed up, but he was still in his fishing clothes.

Eliza spoke first. 'Thank you for helping me catch that salmon. We had it for tea last night.'

'That's okay,' said Jake. He fumbled in his pocket and pulled out the bike valves. 'These are for you,' he said.

'They are the expensive type,' said Eliza.

'I didn't pay for them. I found them at the dump,' Jake explained.

'Do all the presents you give girls come from the dump?' Eliza giggled.

'It's not a present,' said Jake. 'I am replacing the valves you gave me.'

'But they weren't my valves,' said Eliza. 'They were valves I took from my brother's bike, while he was taking the valves from yours.'

'But you must be in trouble for taking your brother's valves.'

'No, because he thinks it was you who took them.'

'I never had a chance to do that,' said Jake.

'I know,' said Eliza, 'but my brother doesn't like you, and he likes to blame people he doesn't like.'

Ben shook his head. 'That all sounds very confusing to me,' he said.

Jake put the valves back in his pocket and changed the subject. 'How come you go to the Old Jetty every morning?' he asked her.

'So, you have noticed then?'

'Er, um, yes. Your yellow hat stands out from a long way off. I can see it when I am fishing.'

'But you would need something like a telescope to see my hat from that far away.'

'Why would I have something like that?' Jake asked.

Ben felt compelled to interrupt. 'That is the exact same question Boof asked me yesterday. He said you were looking at the Old Jetty with some sort of binoculars while you were fishing.'

Thanks to Ben, Jake's awkwardness went up a notch, and he needed a new subject to talk about. 'How come you have such useless fishing gear?' he asked Eliza, which was not how he had planned to raise the subject of the present he had for her.

Ben rolled his eyes but stayed silent, feeling guilty for having already contributed to the deep hole Jake was digging for himself. But Eliza did not appear offended. 'Ivan has all the good stuff,' she said.

'Who is Ivan?' asked Jake.

'Ivan is my twin brother,' said Eliza. 'He wears the number six on his back and thinks you pinched his bike valves. You need to stay clear of him.'

'I thought he was going to throw a punch at me the other day,' said Jake.

'He didn't throw a punch because I was there,' Eliza explained. 'He knows I would have told Dad if he had done that.'

'You would snitch on your brother?'

'I have to,' said Eliza. 'My dad will lose his job if Ivan gets into anymore arguments with the Town Jetty kids, but Ivan is a hothead and might do it anyway.'

'What was the argument about?' asked Jake.

'I don't know,' said Eliza, 'but some Town Jetty kid threw Ivan's bike in the water, and Ivan has vowed to get revenge.'

'It was Hoppy who did that,' said Jake. 'That is what started the jetty war.'

'I guess your dad works for Councillor Cassidy,' Ben interrupted.

'He does, but do you know him?' asked Eliza.

'Yes, but in a bad way,' Ben replied. 'Councillor Cassidy is Hoppy's dad, and he likes to control what happens in this town and takes vengeance on anyone who upsets him or his family.'

'That's not fair,' said Eliza.

'I think it is also unfair that you go fishing with such bad fishing gear,' said Jake, seizing the opportunity to return to that subject. 'I could give you some better stuff if you like.'

'Why would you give me fishing gear?'

'It's my old stuff I thought Mum had thrown out.'

'But I couldn't take it.'

'Why not?'

'People would ask where I got it, and I couldn't tell them that a Town Jetty kid gave it to me.'

Everyone thought for a moment and then Ben had an idea. 'How would you like to paint the back fence of the shop?' he asked Eliza. 'You could say that I gave you the gear as payment for the job.'

'I could help,' Jake added.

'Maybe I could,' said Eliza, 'but I have never painted a fence before.'

'Neither have I,' said Jake.

Ben reconsidered. 'Perhaps it's not a good idea,' he said.

'No, I will do it,' said Jake.

'But Jake, you are the one giving away the fishing gear,' chuckled Ben.

'I guess we could do it together,' said Eliza, 'but it must be kept a secret from everyone.'

'That's right,' said Jake. 'People must never know that you and I are friends.'

'We are friends?' queried Eliza.

'Aren't we?' Jake replied.

'Yes, I think we are,' Eliza said with a giggle.

The matter was settled, and Ben had two painters ready to start work the next day.

The kids left the shop, each going their separate ways, leaving a smiling Ben. Never did he think he would ever be the matchmaker between two twelve-year-old kids, but Jake was never going to get the job done on his own.

11

PAINTING THE FENCE

Ben's two painters arrived the following afternoon, ready to start work. Jake got there first and had begun stirring the paint by the time Eliza arrived. 'What colour is it?' she asked.

'I am not sure,' said Jake. 'It's a mixture of Ben's old cans and is all different colours, but I think it is coming out brown.'

'I don't like brown,' said Eliza.

'What is your favourite colour?' asked Jake.

'Guess.'

'Yellow.'

'How did you guess?'

'Just lucky.'

'So, what is your favourite colour?' asked Eliza.

'Yellow.'

'We can't both have the same favourite colour.'

'Yes, we can. We can share.'

'But I thought boys only liked yucky colours like brown.'

'No. I hate brown.'

'Me too,' said Eliza.

Jake picked up the brush and slapped a splodge of brown onto the fence, some of which began to run down the galvanized iron.

'Where is my brush?' asked Eliza.

'Ben only gave us the one.'

'But he has a shop full of brushes. There must be another brush somewhere. I'm going to ask him.' She popped her head through the back door of the shop. 'Hey, Mister Shopkeeper, do I get a brush too?' she asked.

'You can call me Ben, and Jake is using your brush, but he is only your helper. You are the one getting paid for the job.'

'So, that makes me the boss then?'

'Sure does.'

'Good. I will tell him.' She strode back to Jake and broke the news. 'Ben says I am the boss, and I want the brush,' she announced.

'But you will get paint on you.'

'These are my fishing overalls and I want to get paint on them.'

'Why?'

'That will be proof that Ben gave me the fishing gear for painting his fence. I will have matching paint on my overalls.'

'But no one sees Ben's back fence.'

'If people don't believe me, I will bring them out here and show them.'

'Well, I'm doing some of the painting too.'

'That would be a bad idea,' said Eliza.

'Why?'

'If people see the same paint on your clothes, they will know you helped me.'

That was the moment Jake realised that Eliza was destined to become either the world's greatest lawyer or a notorious criminal master mind. He handed her the brush, but then wondered why she began going over the part he had already done. 'I've already done that bit,' he said.

'You put too much paint on it,' she replied. 'I have to sop some of it up to stop it running down the fence.'

'Who taught you to paint?' asked Jake.

'Never painted before in my life,' said Eliza, 'but it just seems like common sense to me.'

Jake seldom talked to girls and had no idea what things they liked to talk about. Added to this, Eliza seemed so self-confident and assured. 'Did you hear about the circus coming to town?' he asked, thinking that might be a subject of common interest.

'No. When is it coming?' she said.

'I heard the trucks will be here tomorrow, and the big top will be going up in the middle of the Workers Village Sports Field. Perhaps I might see you there tomorrow afternoon.'

'Perhaps, but people might see us there together.'

'How come?'

'Some of the Old Jetty kids might be there, and if they see me with you, they will kick me out of the gang. If that happens, Dad won't be happy because I won't be able to keep an eye on Ivan. But maybe you could watch from a distance and wait until I am alone.'

'How could I do that?' Jake asked.

'Use your binoculars,' she giggled.

Jake had hoped that she had forgotten about the binocular story, but apparently not. 'They are opera glasses,' he growled. 'They fold up in my pocket and are not very powerful.'

'Just strong enough to see things at the opera, I suppose.'

'That's right.'

'So, how often do you go?'

'Go where?'

'To the opera.'

'Never.'

'You only use them for fishing then?'

'That's right.'

'And you could see my yellow hat in the distance with them?'

'Sort of.'

'Like only when you looked very hard.' giggled Eliza, but then she sensed that her teasing was going too far. 'I wish I had a pair of fold up opera glasses like yours,' she said, changing her tone. 'They seem like a very good idea.'

'They are,' said Jake, and then he turned the conversation back to the circus. 'I am going to try for a job at the circus,' he said. 'I've heard they want kids to sell sweets and stuff like that.'

'Do you think a girl could get a job there?'

'Maybe, but some of the jobs aren't good. I knew a kid once who had to clean up animal pooh.'

'I would do that if they paid me enough money,' said Eliza. 'How much did he get paid?'

'I don't think he ever got paid. I think they conned him.'

'Well, I'm going to try because I'm saving up.'

'What are you saving for?'

'Jodhpurs.'

'You mean those fancy, horse riding pants?'

'Yes, and they are not fancy. Some soldiers have them as part of their uniform, even if they only ride on motorbikes.'

'But you're not a soldier and you don't have a horse or a motorbike.'

'They are the fashion,' said Eliza. 'All the kids were wearing them last winter. How come you never noticed.'

'I was at boarding school.'

'You go to boarding school?'

'Yes.'

'That means your dad is rich.'

'No. Grandpa sends me there on a special scholarship.'

'You must be smart then.'

'Not really. My grandpa was once headmaster of the college, and he arranged a special scholarship for me.'

'What sort of scholarship?'

'A chess scholarship.'

'You play chess?'

'I have to in order to keep my scholarship.'

'Perhaps we could have a game,' said Eliza, 'but you will probably win, because I don't have a chess scholarship. I never knew schools gave them out.'

'Grandpa had the college invent one for me,' said Jake, 'but it's embarrassing because the other kids in the chess team think I should not be in it.' Then Jake changed the subject again, for his chess scholarship was not something he liked to talk about. 'What colour jodhpurs are you getting?' he asked.

'Brown.'

'But you hate brown.'

'Brown is the fashionable colour for Jodhpurs.'

'But you only like yellow.'

'Brown goes with yellow, so I can wear my jodhpurs with a yellow top.'

'But kids don't use their own money to buy clothes,' said Jake. 'Their parents buy their clothes, and their mums decide what looks best.'

'Girls like to choose their own clothes.'

'That doesn't sound much fun to me,' Jake chuckled.

'That's because you are not a girl. Girls grow up quicker than boys.'

'They don't. Everyone grows up the same.'

Jake was entering territory he knew nothing about and was arguing over things he thought silly. He liked Eliza but would have to stop arguing, or their brief friendship would be no more. Fortunately, Eliza was thinking the same.

'Sorry,' she said. 'I was just saying what the other girls say. I don't really know myself.'

'Me neither,' said Jake. 'Maybe girls do grow up quicker, but boys must catch up at some time. I really don't care.'

'I don't think it matters,' said Eliza. 'I just want to hurry up and finish this fence so you can show me the fishing gear you have for me.'

Fortunately, it was not a very big fence, and the job was soon done. Ben came out to inspect the work. 'Good job,' he said. 'Eliza could get a job as a painter any time.'

'Do you think a circus would have a job for a painter?' asked Eliza.

'Probably not,' said Ben. 'I think they do that sort of thing themselves, but it is time for me to pay you for your labour.'

Ben went into the shop and reached behind the counter, then handed Eliza the rod and reel. 'I must say,' he said, turning his attention to Jake, 'your old fishing gear has a lot of newness about it. This reel is so well cleaned and oiled, and the rod appears to have been freshly varnished. I can't believe you thought your mother might throw them out.'

Yet again, Jake felt embarrassed. He had probably gone overboard with his renovation, but Eliza was flattered. Jake was the first boy who had ever paid her attention, let alone given her such a nice gift. 'Thank you so much,' she said. 'The other kids are already upset because I caught a salmon. Wait till they see my new fishing gear. I am going to become the best fisherperson on the jetty.'

She gave Jake a peck on the cheek, which stunned him more than any blow he had ever taken in a fight. 'Sorry, I won't do that again,' Eliza giggled.

Jake stood in silence, holding his jaw, while Ben smiled. Eliza joined the two sections of rod together and began waving it like a sword. 'Best do that outside,' said Ben.

The kids went out to the footpath but then Ben called out, 'Hey, you two, the job isn't finished. Someone has to clean the brush.'

'I will do it,' said Jake. 'It's getting late, and Eliza has further to go than me.'

'Thanks,' said Eliza. 'I will watch out for you at the circus tomorrow.' Then she hopped on her bike, eager to show her family her new fishing gear.

12

GORILLA BOY

When Jake arrived at the sports field the next day, he found it had been transformed into a place of unimaginable excitement. Normally, it was little more than a paddock of mowed grass on which stood a pair of goal posts, and any plan to develop it beyond that was still well into the future. But trucks had arrived in the night, each towing a cage, caravan, or animal float, and the place had become a carnival wonderland. Centre to it all was a massive tent, its walls adorned with red and white stripes. Then close to the tent were the circus animals, some of which lounged in barred cages, while three elephants stood chained to the ground. Further away, ponies grazed in a makeshift corral.

The circus people were rushing about, putting the finishing touches on various stalls, while dodging kids that were everywhere. Jake stood on the footpath and peered through the wire fence, but Eliza was not one of the kids. His heart sank. It appeared that she had decided not to come, which meant that she was not that eager to be his friend after all. He wondered what he had done to upset her, or perhaps he was just the type of person no one liked. *Once and outsider, always an outsider*, he thought.

Jake pushed aside his disappointment, for he was not going to let the opportunity of a visiting circus go to waste. He joined the kids gathered at the animal cages, where all were hoping to see one animal in particular, the gorilla. The gorilla was the most awesome of all wild creatures, and any jungle picture worth seeing always featured this fearsome ape, but no one had ever seen the real thing. However, the circus boasted that it had one that performed in every show.

A circus worker walked up to the lion's cage and turned to the kids. 'You have to come and see the show,' he said. 'That big fellow in the corner wants to eat me, but I keep him under control.'

'Are you the lion tamer?' came a question.

'That's me, and we are here for four days. Get your parents to bring you along and watch me put these man eaters through their tricks.'

'Where is the gorilla?' asked Jake.

'Can't tell you that, son. We keep him locked away in a safe place. He is too dangerous to have here with the other animals.'

Jake was disappointed because he wanted to see the gorilla, but then his thoughts returned to Eliza. Perhaps she had sneaked into the big top, so he peeped inside. A man shouted from above. 'Hey, Gorilla Boy, go tell your old man to get his butt in here.'

Jake thought for a moment that the man was shouting to him, but then he saw Gorilla Boy. He was nearby and had what appeared to be rolled up circus posters under his arm. 'Say please, you clown,' shouted Gorilla Boy. He had a heavy accent which Jake thought could have had its origins in some jungle tribe.

'Get him now or there won't be any red lights for tonight's performance,' shouted the man.

Gorilla Boy left and Jake followed. He had accidently come across a clue that none of the other kids knew about. The man had called him Gorilla Boy, which meant he knew something about the gorilla. Perhaps he was heading for the gorilla's secret location right now.

Jake's hunch turned out to be partly correct, for the boy disappeared into a caravan that had a large gorilla painted on the side. It was obviously the caravan of the gorilla's trainer and perhaps the gorilla was close by. A man came out of the caravan and brushed past Jake. He was unshaven and in need of a shower. Jake thought he might be the gorilla's trainer, but he saw no point in following him because he was probably off to fix some lights. But then Gorilla Boy came out, still holding the rolled-up posters, and he now had a jar and a paint brush as well.

'Excuse me,' said Jake. 'Can you tell me where I can find the gorilla?'

Gorilla Boy glared at him, then said in broken English. 'This place private. Get lost.'

Jake took an instant dislike to Gorilla Boy but did not reply. He watched him walk behind the caravan. *I bet that is where they keep the gorilla,* he thought. He followed, but what he found was not what he expected. Gorilla Boy was behind the caravan, and he was talking to Eliza.

Eliza saw Jake and shouted, 'Hi, Jake. I've got a job.'

Gorilla Boy turned and saw Jake. 'You friends?' he asked.

'Yes,' said Jake.

'You both want job?'

'What is it?' Jake asked.

'Put posters around town. We pay.'

'How much?' asked Jake.

'Depends. You do good job.'

Jake thought the reply was far from satisfactory, but Eliza was more trusting. 'We will take the job,' she said.

'Okay, Missy. I give you job because I like you.'

'Him too?' asked Eliza, pointing to Jake.

'Okay. Him job too. Come before Sunday show. We pay.'

'Is the man fixing the lights really a clown?' asked Jake.

'Him clown, electrician, safety marshal. Has gun if animals escape.'

'Has an animal ever escaped?' asked Jake.

'Gorilla stronger every day. Might break chain.'

'That certainly sounds dangerous,' said Eliza.

'Yes, Missy. Circus people very brave.' He handed the posters to Eliza and the jar and brush to Jake.

'What is this for?' Jake asked.

'Stick posters to wall,' said Gorilla Boy. 'Very obvious.'

Jake was still finding it hard to like Gorilla Boy, but Eliza seemed impressed by him. They watched him as he swaggered back to the big top.

'I couldn't find you,' said Jake. 'I thought you would be wearing your yellow hat.'

'My yellow hat stands out, and I don't want people to see me here,' she replied. 'Besides, I do have other hats you know, it's just that I like the yellow one best.' They peered around the corner of the caravan. 'We should leave,' she said. 'Some of the Old Jetty Gang are over by the lion's cage.'

'But I haven't had a look around yet,' said Jake.

'Then stay,' she replied, 'but I must go. We can't be seen here together.'

Jake had to decide. Does he choose a rare opportunity to see a circus set up, or does he go with Eliza? 'Did you just come here to get a job?' he asked.

'No. I mainly came here because you said you would be here,' she said. 'It just so happened that Gorilla Boy saw me and asked me if I wanted the job.'

Her answer was all that Jake could have hoped for. For once, someone was dashing his *always an outsider* theory. She had come to see him, and he could not help but smile as he followed her towards a broken section of fence. 'Why are we going this way?' he asked.

'There are too many people by the gate,' she said. 'Someone might see us together.'

They left the sports field and began the serious business of putting up posters. It was their first paid job, and they would be working as a team. 'You can be in charge of the paint brush and glue, and I will put up the posters,' said Eliza.

Eliza was being the boss again, but Jake was happy to go along because it was another argument he was never going to win. Gorilla Boy had given her the job. Like before, he was just the helper. 'Do you think we will get paid?' he asked.

'I think so,' she said.

'But the kid who shovelled animal pooh never got paid.'

'I know,' shrugged Eliza, 'but that was probably a different circus, and besides, Gorilla Boy has an honest face and I think he's kind of cute.'

Jake felt a touch of jealousy.

13

THE POSTER JOB

The circus's newly appointed poster team headed for the town centre, looking for places to put up posters. They stopped at the church, for it had an excellent notice board that people often looked at. 'I think we should put one up here,' said Eliza.

'But what if God is watching?' cautioned Jake.

'Do you think God goes around spying on people?'

'I can't say.'

'Why not?'

'He might be listening.'

'I don't think the Ten Commandments mention anything about posters,' said Eliza.

'So, we would not be breaking the law then?' questioned Jake.

'If it were against the law, the Bible would say so,' Eliza reasoned.

Jake had no idea what the Bible had to say about sticking up circus posters, but Eliza seemed more informed on the subject, so he went along with whatever she thought. However, the notice board was already full, which meant one of the notices had to be covered. 'Which one should we cover?' he asked.

'The Thursday Ladies Get-together,' Eliza suggested.

'Why?'

'Because no one ever reads it.'

'How do you know?'

'Because it's Thursday and no one is here.'

'I think we should cover the Sunday School notice,' said Jake.

'Why?'

'Because I don't like Sunday School.'

'Okay.'

Jake slapped paste over the chosen notice but then hesitated. He thought about Miss Brown. He was already in her bad books. What would happen if she found out that he had covered her notice. 'Are you sure this is not against the law?' he asked again.

'The circus would not give us this job if it were against the law,' said Eliza.

Eliza seemed to know all the answers and took responsibility for things, such as keeping an eye on her brother. But Jake was less self-assured. 'Perhaps we shouldn't put a poster here,' he said.

'Too late now,' said Eliza. 'You have already slapped on the paste, and we will run out if we start wasting it.'

She whacked a poster over Miss Brown's notice and then stood back to admire her work. 'I think that clown's face brightens up the whole notice board,' she said. 'I wouldn't be surprised if the church people leave it there even after the circus has gone.'

The kids set off to find the next good spot to put a poster, but then they looked back. Bottles had appeared from nowhere and was looking at the notice board. He shook his head and then ripped down their poster, after which he wiped the wet paste off the board with his sleeve.

Their job had gotten off to a bad start, but the next few posters went up with no such interference. The town hall, the railway station, the public toilets, and even the picture theatre, were all adorned with a circus poster.

'Let's ask Ben if we can paste one on his front window,' said Eliza.

'How come we have to ask Ben when we haven't asked anyone else?' said Jake. 'Are you sure we are not breaking the law?'

'Gorilla Boy would have warned us if that were the case,' Eliza replied.

They walked into Ben's shop. 'Hi, Ben, can we paste a circus poster on your front window?' Jake asked.

'Sure,' was the friendly reply, 'but you will have to remove it and clean the glass once the circus leaves town.'

'We will,' said Eliza, but then Ben had a warning.

'It's good that you asked for my permission because it's against the law to put up posters otherwise.'

'You mean we can't put a sign in a shop window without permission?' said Eliza.

'No,' said Ben. 'You can't put posters up anywhere without permission. Some call it vandalism.'

Eliza appeared a little worried. 'Oh dear, the circus didn't warn us about that. I don't want to get caught breaking the law,' she said.

'Why are you putting up posters then?' Ben asked.

'The circus is going to pay us.'

'I see,' was Ben's reply. 'I can only wish you luck with that one.'

It appeared that Eliza was the only one who thought they would ever see money for the project, but Jake did not care, he was simply happy to be helping her. Then he had an idea. 'I will put up the posters,' he said. 'You can pretend to just be watching.'

'That means you will be taking all the risks,' said Eliza.

'It won't be a risk,' Jake replied. 'I know all the hiding spots around here. Your job can be to look out for Biggles and warn me if you see him coming.'

Biggles was the name the kids gave Police Officer Biggs. They reckoned that whenever he rode his motorbike, he considered himself to be the earth-bound version of the famous airman.

'Okay. If we have to split up, I will meet you under the Old Jetty tomorrow afternoon,' said Eliza.

'Sounds like Jake wants to be a hero,' laughed Ben, which was close to the truth. Gorilla Boy was currently the number one hero in Eliza's eyes, which was something Jake was keen to change. However, he was unaware that Councillor Cassidy had already lodged a complaint about the poster on the town hall, and Biggles was already on the case.

14

IN TROUBLE WITH THE LAW

The kids left Ben's shop and walked towards the beach, but then they heard Biggles' motorbike. Jake grabbed everything from Eliza. 'Just keep walking,' he said as he ran off. But it was too late, because Biggles saw him bolting up the street with the posters under his arm. He gave chase, but Jake knew the lay of the land and ran up stairs that led to the town lookout. It was a path that no motorbike could follow.

Biggles pulled up beside Eliza. 'Who is that kid running up those stairs?' he asked.

'I have no idea,' she replied, which gave her something in common with Jake's mum, for both had now lied to the law to protect Jake.

Jake reached the lookout and then ran down a second set of steps that led to the esplanade. He looked about. The coast was clear, and not far away, the Town Jetty Gang was gathered outside Hoppy's house. He sprinted the short distance and joined them. 'Hi,' said Boof, who was the only one to see him arrive. The rest were looking at something never seen before. A man was putting a TV antenna on Hoppy's roof.

'What is going on?' asked Jake.

'Hoppy's dad is getting a TV,' said Boof.

'But it could be another two years before the town gets TV,' said Jake.

'I know,' Boof replied, 'but Hoppy's dad thinks he might get a bit of a picture if he points the antennae towards Melbourne.'

It was then that Jake heard the police motorbike heading towards them. Sure enough, Biggles pulled up not far from the kids.

'Quick, Boof, hide these,' said Jake.

Boof was on his weekly paper round and had rolled-up newspapers in the front carry basket of his bike. Jake put the posters in with them. 'Thanks, Boof,' he said. 'Biggles will never find them in there.'

'Why is Biggles looking for them?' asked Boof.

'They are circus posters and Biggles is chasing me because I was putting them up. It's against the law to put up posters.'

'Cool,' said Boof, 'but did he recognise you?'

'I am not sure,' said Jake.

Biggles walked up to the kids. 'Attention, you lot,' he said in a voice of authority. 'Have any of you seen a kid carrying rolled up posters?'

No one answered, for all had been looking up at Hoppy's roof. Then Biggles spotted the jar of paste which Jake had put on the footpath. 'One of you kids is the guilty party,' he said. 'Who put that jar on the footpath?'

Again, no one had seen what had happened.

'One of you is hiding a roll of posters,' Biggles growled, but then Hoppy came out of the house.

'Excuse me, Officer Biggs,' said Hoppy. 'Dad says you should come inside and see our new TV.'

Biggles' face lit up. 'Thank you, Gerald, I would love to see it. I have never seen a real TV. Can you get a picture on it?'

'No, just dots.'

Biggles went into the house, which was Jake's chance to get away, but Jake did not always make good choices, and Biggles soon returned. He went straight to Boof's bike and pulled out the posters. 'What is your name, lad?' he snapped. 'Your police record starts as of now.'

Jake interrupted. 'Don't ask him. It's my name you want, not his.'

'I don't need your name, Jake Jones. I already know your name. You are already on my watch list.'

'No,' said Jake. 'I am the one who was putting up posters. Boof doesn't even know that I just put them in his basket.'

Jake looked to an upstairs window of the house and saw the smiling face of Hoppy looking down. It was obvious that Hoppy had seen him hide the posters and had snitched.

Biggles turned his attention to Jake. 'I am putting this incident on your record, Jones. You need to change your ways, or you will find yourself in juvenile court.'

Jake walked home, minus the paste and posters, but worse was to come. He turned into his street and saw Biggles riding away from his house. News of his lawbreaking had preceded him. His mum had already been told and he was about to be grounded again. 'Hi, Mum,' he said as he walked through the door.

'Hi, Sweetie,' said his mum, and then she paused before saying, 'Officer Biggs has just been to see me again.'

'What did he want?' asked Jake.

'He said you have been putting up circus posters.'

'I didn't know it was against the law,' Jake pleaded.

'Neither did I,' said his mum, 'and I remember how it was when I was a girl. Seeing circus posters about town was one of the exciting things that happened when a circus came to town. I told Officer Biggs that he was a killjoy and should be ashamed of himself. He needed to be out chasing real criminals rather than picking on innocent children.'

Jake was not grounded, and he thought that he had to be the luckiest of kids because he had the greatest mum in the whole world.

15

A SECRET MEETING

It was early afternoon when Jake arrived at the Old Jetty. Eliza had not set a time, but he wanted to make sure that he did not keep her waiting. He hid his bike in a bush some distance away and walked along the beach, keeping out of sight by staying close to the seawall. He had wondered why Eliza would pick a meeting place in the middle of his enemies' territory, but once he got there, he saw the reason. The winter storms had left seaweed piled high under the jetty, and seaweed was excellent for building seaweed forts. This versatile material could be piled into a circle, and people going past would think they were seeing just a heap of seaweed, not realising that it was the walls of a fort that hid its occupants within.

The section of seawall that ran beneath the jetty had always held a fascination for Jake, for it had a wooden door built into it. No one knew what lay on the other side of the door, but the only thing that should ever be behind a seawall was dirt. Jake called it *The Mystery Door* and guessed that it was an entrance to a tunnel, but he could not figure out where the tunnel would be heading. He had once asked Ben about the door, but Ben did not know the answer. He said that the jetty had been used by the Army during the war, and that was when the door appeared, but no one knew its purpose, and since the war, the Army had kept it locked.

Jake built a circular fort with walls high enough to hide behind, and Eliza arrived just as the last lump of seaweed was being put into place.

'You must have got here early,' she said.

'Well, you are early too.'

'Not as early as you.'

'I had to find somewhere to hide my bike, so I got here early,' explained Jake.

'Do you like my secret place?' asked Eliza. 'I come here if I want to get away from people, but sorry about the pong.'

'What pong?'

'The rotting seaweed.'

'That is just normal beach smell to me,' said Jake. 'I actually miss that smell when I am at boarding school.'

'That smell keeps most people away,' explained Eliza. 'That is what makes this a good secret hiding place.'

'I am surprised that a girl would think that smell was okay,' said Jake.

'Why?'

'Girls aren't as tough as boys.'

Eliza was not impressed. 'Who changed your nappies when you were a baby?' she asked.

'Can't remember.'

'I bet your dad didn't do it.'

'Probably not.'

'Who cleaned up the last time you chucked?'

'Probably Mum.'

'I bet your mum also picks up dog pooh from your front lawn.'

'Okay, can I just say that girls aren't as strong as boys?'

'Sure, but never say we are not as tough.'

'Fair enough,' agreed Jake. 'Sorry I messed up with the posters yesterday.'

'What do you mean?'

'I didn't put anymore up after I left you. Biggles caught me.'

'Stop teasing,' laughed Eliza. 'My big brother tells me that there are posters all over town. You must have put them up.

'It wasn't me. Someone else must have done it.'

'I wondered about that,' said Eliza. 'It was done in the early hours of the morning when you would have been in bed.'

'How do you know?' asked Jake.

'My big brother told me there were no posters when he came home from the pictures last night, but they were on all the bus stops this morning.'

'The circus people must have done it when no one was about,' said Jake. 'They probably do it then because they know it is against the law.'

'They still have to pay us for the ones we did,' said Eliza, 'and I am going to tell Gorilla Boy that I am not happy with him. He should have warned us that it was against the law.'

Jake smiled to himself. Gorilla Boy had fallen off his pedestal.

'Are you in trouble with the law now?' asked Eliza.

'No,' said Jake. 'Biggles is always catching kids for doing things, but he just gives out warnings. What picture did your brother see?'

'"Rock around the Clock", and I want to see it too,' said Eliza.

'Isn't it just dancing and stuff?'

'Mainly.'

'Does anyone get shot?'

'I don't think so.'

'What about a plane crash?'

'I don't think there are planes in it.'

'How about a gorilla, like in Tarzan?'

'No. They only have gorillas in jungle pictures.'

Jake could not imagine why they would make a picture without guns, planes, wild animals, or pirates. 'Is it really just music and dancing?' he asked.

'It's about Rock and Roll, like in the song, "Rock around the Clock".'

'I know the song,' said Jake. 'I love that song, but how could a song be a picture?'

'I don't know,' said Eliza. 'That is why I want to see it. They say it makes you want to dance.'

'I don't think a picture would make me want to dance,' said Jake, who was finding it hard to understand the concept.

'I heard that people dance in the aisles while the picture is on,' explained Eliza.

Jake had his doubts. 'I don't think people are allowed to do that,' he said.

'Why don't we see it and find out,' Eliza suggested.

'You mean like go together?'

'Yes.'

'What if we get seen?'

'You could sneak in after the show starts and meet me in there,' she said.

'But I might miss a cartoon.'

'Alright, I will be the one who sneaks in after the show starts.'

'But do you have the money to buy a ticket?' he asked.

'I get a shilling a week pocket money for doing the dishes and watering the garden. How about you?'

'I get two shillings a week.'

'What do you have to do for that?' asked Eliza.

'Keep my room tidy.'

'In other words, I get a shilling a week for doing jobs, while you get two shillings a week as a bribe.'

'What do you mean?'

'Keeping your room tidy is not a job. It is something you should be doing without being paid.'

'Funny. That is what my mum says too. You and Mum would probably get along well together.'

'That is because girls all think the same way,' said Eliza.

'You mean girls think differently to boys?'

'Yes, and we need to plan how to go to the pictures without being seen.'

Jake was discovering that girls were far more complex than he had imagined. 'What is there to plan?' he asked.

'We need to work out the best place to sit, and it has to be a place where I can find you in the dark. I suggest you sit in the middle of the back row, and you should get to your seat from the left-hand aisle.'

'Why the left-hand aisle?'

'Because I will get there from the right-hand aisle.'

'Why?'

'Because if there is anyone there that we know, they will only ever see one of us, so they will never know that we are there together.'

Jake was impressed by Eliza's planning skills and how she was prepared to be the one who sacrificed seeing the cartoon. He knew of no other kid with such impressive qualities. 'I guess we have to sit in the seats made for the big people,' he said.

'Why would you say that?'

'Because the seats in the back row are twice as wide as the rest.'

'I think they call them loveseats,' giggled Eliza.

'Yuck!' exclaimed Jake. 'Why would they call them that?'

'So that couples can sit in them together, but I want a whole seat to myself.'

'So do I,' said Jake.

Jake wondered if Eliza had ever used her problem-solving skills to solve the mystery of the door behind them. 'I wonder why that door never gets used,' he said.

'They still use it,' she replied.

'Who?'

'I don't know who, but when seaweed builds up against the wall, someone always clears it away from the doorway.'

'Really?'

'Yes. Look for yourself. There is seaweed against the wall, but the doorway is clear.'

Eliza was right. *She would make a good detective,* thought Jake, and so he asked, 'How often do you think the door gets used?'

'I don't know,' she said, 'but I think it gets used at night.'

Jake and Eliza spent the rest of the day talking about the kids at school, their favourite things, and what song would be top of the Hit Parade that week. All too soon it was time to go, each going their separate way, Jake along the seawall and Eliza up the stairs to the jetty.

16

THE PICTURES

The next day was Saturday, and Jake was off to the Saturday afternoon matinee. 'Will Boof be there?' his mum asked as he left.

'Maybe.'

'But you always sit with Boof at the pictures.'

'Not always.'

'But who are you going to sit with if Boof isn't there?'

'Why is it important who I sit with?'

'Because you always sit with Boof, and I don't want you sitting next to a stranger.'

I should have just said I was going with Boof, thought Jake. *Now I've made it complicated for myself.* 'I am going with a new friend,' he said.

'What is his name?'

Jake did not want his mum to know that he was going with a girl, not that she would have minded, but he would be in trouble if his dad found out. His dad did not approve of Jake playing with girls and said it would turn him into a sissy. 'Doolittle,' Jake replied.

'That's an odd name for a boy. What does he do?' asked his mum.

'Not much,' said Jake. 'That is probably how come the name.'

'You will have to bring Doolittle home for me to meet sometime.'

'Okay,' Jake replied, and then he raced out the door before his mum could ask another question.

A short time later, he arrived at the theatre and saw Eliza on the other side of the road. She was looking in the window of a motorbike shop, and she gave him a quick wave and he waved back. Then he bought a ticket and went into the theatre. Luckily, the big people seats were all empty because the Saturday afternoon crowd always sat nearer the front.

The theatre also had upstairs seating, but kids were not allowed up there without an adult. It was a wise precaution management took to prevent downstairs patrons from being bombed by small objects dropping from above. But management could do nothing about Jaffers being rolled along the floor other than to put up their price in the kiosk. Fortunately, only the kids with rich parents could afford to buy these yummy, candy-coated balls of chocolate.

Jake sat in the middle of the back row and put his jacket on the seat beside him. The lights dimmed, the curtains opened, and Her Majesty appeared on the screen, riding a horse to the accompaniment of her anthem, "God Save the Queen". Then came a newsreel and Jake could only marvel at how he was watching something that happened on the other side of the world only a few days before. He was so lucky to be living in such modern times, an opinion reinforced when one story told how America hoped to soon launch its first satellite into space.

It was while the newsreel was running that a couple came in, and an usher shone a torch along the back row. They chose the big person's seat next to Jake and both squashed into it. *Yuk* thought Jake.

Next on the program was a Tom and Jerry cartoon. 'Seen it!' yelled the audience, which was the reception every cartoon got at a Saturday afternoon matinee. The fact was, the theatre recycled its cartoons on a regular basis, but the kids never tired of seeing them, despite their protests.

Then the usher's torch flashed again. Eliza was being shown to her seat.

'Are you sitting with that boy?' asked the usher.

'No way,' said Eliza. 'I just like a big seat all to myself because it has lots of room.'

'So do I,' the usher giggled.

Eliza sat down. 'Hi, Jake,' she whispered.

'Hi, Eliza. Did you see a motorbike you would like to buy?'

'I was only pretending to look at them,' she said, still keeping her voice low. 'Just making sure that no one saw me, but I did see a motorbike like my big brother's. It is parked out the front.'

She glanced across to the person sitting next to Jake. Shock, horror, it was her big brother, Sam, and he was cosied up to a girl. Eliza could not believe her bad luck. *Why is Sam seeing the same picture again?* she thought. She sank back into her seat and tugged on Jake's sleeve. 'We have to move,' she whispered, but at that moment, Tom made a futile attempt to clobber Jerry. A loud crash thundered through the theatre.

Jake raised his voice. 'Pardon, Eliza,' he said.

Sam heard the mention of his sister's name and leant forward, and Eliza had nowhere to hide. In the flicker of the theatre light, he saw his sister huddled behind Jake.

'Hi, Sam,' she said, her voice far less confident than usual.

Neither spoke for a few seconds, and then Sam said, 'Please don't tell Mum and Dad that I am here with Violet.'

Eliza had wondered why the family had never met Sam's girlfriend but had not realised that Sam was deliberately keeping her identity a secret. 'I will keep your secret if you keep mine,' she said. 'This is my friend Jake.'

'Hi, Jake.'

'Hi, Sam.'

Everyone settled down to watch the first feature which was much to Jake's liking, for there were gunfights from start to finish. Then came the interval. The lights came on and it was time for Jake and Eliza to become invisible. Sam got up to buy treats at the kiosk.

'I am going to sit with Violet while the lights are on,' said Eliza.

'Good idea,' said Violet. 'Jake can follow Sam out to the kiosk.'

'No point,' said Jake. 'I've got no more money.'

'Sam, you should buy them something,' said Violet.

'Okay.'

Jake thought he might remain sitting in his oversized seat, but then he gave it more thought. His newly acquired knowledge that it was a loveseat, not a big person's seat, made him feel uncomfortable. He would not like someone like Hoppy seeing him in a loveseat, so he got up and followed Sam.

Once the girls were together, Eliza asked Violet why she and Sam had to be a secret.

'I'm Catholic,' she said.

'Oh, I see,' said Eliza. 'That certainly would not go well with Mum and Dad.'

'No,' said Violet. 'Sam wouldn't go well with my folks either. They say Hell would have to freeze over before I would be allowed to go out with a Protestant.'

'Stupid grownups,' said Eliza.

'I agree,' said Violet. 'So is Jake a Catholic too?'

'No.'

'So, what is the problem?'

'There is a war going on between the jetty kids and I am on one side and Jake is on the other.' Then she added, 'I also have a feeling that Jake's parents don't want him to have a girlfriend.'

'Is Jake your boyfriend?' asked Violet.

'Not really,' said Eliza. 'We just like doing stuff together.'

Sam returned with ice-creams for himself and Violet, and a packet of Lifesavers for Eliza and Jake to share.

'Thanks, Sam,' said Eliza, knowing that her brother's offering was a token bribe for her silence.

The lights faded and the feature began, and soon the theatre was shaking to the beat of Rock and Roll, but Eliza was disappointed. No one was jiving in the aisles, but then Violet said, 'Come on, Sam, we jived last time.'

'But no one is doing it now,' said Sam.

'That is because the place is full of kids, not teenagers.'

'I'm a kid and I want to jive,' said Eliza. 'Let's jive, Jake. No one will see us in the dark back here.'

'Can't jive,' said Jake.

'Hey, Eliza, let's jive together,' said Violet. 'The two wallflowers can just watch.'

The girls got up and jived in the aisle, while the boys stayed stuck in their seats.

'Why aren't you dancing?' Jake asked Sam.

'Not enough people doing it. I only dance in a crowd when people take no notice, but what about you?'

'Same reason,' said Jake.

17

A SLOW WALK HOME

Time passed quickly that afternoon, and before they knew it, the picture was coming to an end. Sam whispered to Jake, 'Violet and I are leaving before the lights come on.'

'Okay,' said Jake, not thinking that Eliza and he should be doing the same.

The picture ended, the curtains closed, and the lights came on. 'Where are Sam and Violet?' asked Eliza.

'Gone. Sam said they had to leave while the theatre was still dark.'

'We should have gone too,' said Eliza, but it was too late. Kids were already leaving their seats and walking towards them. Quick thinking was needed. 'Look for something on the floor,' said Eliza.

'Like what?' asked Jake.

'Anything. Just keep your head low and start crawling about down there.'

Jake did as Eliza suggested, while she pretended to be looking for something stuck behind her seat. Once the rush was over, she said, 'You can come up now.'

Jake got to his feet and began walking towards the front of the theatre.

'Where are you going?' asked Eliza. 'The exit is the other way.'

'I usually go out through the fire-escape,' said Jake. 'It leads to the back lane.' He went to a side door, pushed on the quick release bar, and the door swung open.

'Are we allowed to be doing this?' Eliza asked.

Jake smiled. 'I always go out this way and no one has ever told me I can't do it,' he said.

Moments later, they were outside, walking along the lane. 'You must go to the pictures a lot if you know that trick,' said Eliza.

'No. I only go on Saturdays.'

'That's a lot.'

'Why, how often do you go?'

'I have never been to the pictures on my own before,' Eliza answered. 'Mum sometimes takes me on my birthday because that is a special occasion.'

'I thought kids went to the pictures all the time.'

'Not in my family. My parents are saving to buy a house.'

'But you already have a house.'

'Not really. We live in one of the houses that the Government built for immigrants, but it is too small for us and gets hot in the summer.'

'I didn't realise you lived in one of those places,' said Jake, 'and I am sorry that I didn't have money for the kiosk.'

'That's okay,' Eliza replied as she pulled a coin from her pocket. 'I've got two shillings.'

'Wow. So why didn't you get something at the kiosk?'

'Couldn't.'

'Why not?'

'I only found it down the back of my seat a couple of minutes ago.'

'Lucky,' said Jake. 'I'm hoping to get money when the circus pays us tomorrow, but I doubt that they will. They will claim that they put up most of the posters themselves.'

'They had better pay us,' said Eliza. 'Gorilla Boy owes us. Not telling us that it was breaking the law has gotten you into trouble.'

'Why did your brother leave early?' Jake asked.

'My parents don't approve of Violet,' she replied. 'It's stupid how grownups are always telling us that Catholics and Protestants should each keep to their own.'

'I don't understand it either,' said Jake, 'but Boof thinks us Protestants might be on the wrong side.'

'I didn't know there were sides,' said Eliza. 'What do you mean?'

'Boof thinks that God is on the side of the Catholic kids.'

'How come?'

'Boof says that when he rides his bike to school of a morning, he passes the Catholic kids going the other way because their school is on the other side of town.'

'So?'

'Well, Boof says the wind often comes from the north in the morning. He has to slog into it, but it is a tailwind for the Catholic kids. They go sailing by, pushed by the wind, all the way to school. They hardly have to pedal.'

'But doesn't it even out in the afternoon?'

'No, because the sea breeze comes in and blows from the opposite direction. Boof has to slog into the wind again while the Catholic kids get another free ride home.'

'I don't think God would have planned it that way,' said Eliza. 'I think they just built Boof's school in the wrong place.'

'I think so too,' said Jake, 'but Boof reckons it's unfair.'

'Why didn't you dance today?' asked Eliza.

Jake shook his head. 'I've never been taught to dance.'

'The Sunday School people are running dance classes during the school holidays,' Eliza replied. 'You should go because I will be there.'

'But you don't go to Sunday School.'

'That doesn't matter,' she said. 'The classes are mainly for the kids in the Workers Village, but a couple of the Sunday School girls go there as well.'

'Will Ivan be there?'

'Yes, and that is one of the reasons I go. I keep an eye on him just in case any Town Jetty kids should ever decide to come.'

'But I am a Town Jetty kid,' said Jake. He was liking the idea of learning to dance with Eliza, but she could tell that he was seeing too many problems.

'Don't worry,' she said. 'Ivan won't start any trouble while I am around.'

'But we can't be seen together.'

'That won't be a problem either,' Eliza laughed. 'I will pretend that I don't know you.'

'It still sounds very risky,' said Jake.

'You are afraid to take a risk then?'

Jake shrugged. 'Risks don't bother me. I take my dad's boat out on my own and not many kids do that.'

'That doesn't sound risky to me.'

'Okay. I will go to the dance class if you come out in the boat with me.'

'It's a deal,' said Eliza.

They walked at a snail's pace, watching out for kids that might know them, with the danger of being seen increasing the closer they got to Eliza's home. But fortune favoured them, and they reached her corner without being seen. 'I live in the third house along,' she said, pointing to a row of identical buildings. Then she added, 'See you at the circus tomorrow.'

'Okay,' said Jake.

Eliza left, leaving Jake to watch her skip all the way to her front gate. It had been a day he would never forget.

18

PAY DAY AT THE CIRCUS

Jake had Sunday School the next morning, which he endured, knowing that he would be meeting Eliza at the circus that afternoon. He arrived at the sports field not long before the circus matinee was due to start, expecting to find Eliza waiting by the hole in the fence, but she was not there. He looked towards Gorilla Boy's caravan, but she wasn't there either. Most people were gathered in the sideshow area and were trying their luck at darts, hoopla, or buying treats. Jake had heard that there had been big crowds, but the Sunday crowd was smaller than expected. He wandered over to where most were gathered, partly drawn by the smell of hot donuts, not that he had money to buy them.

Then a voice came from behind. 'Hi, Jake. I have always wanted to ride a real horse.'

Eliza was sitting on a pony, enjoying an elevated view of her surroundings, but the lad in charge of her mount appeared in need of a good night's sleep, and so did his noble steed.

Jake had always thought that circus life would be one great adventure, but those involved in its pony riding enterprise painted a different picture. *Perhaps they are just having a bad day,* he thought, but Eliza was enjoying the experience and that was all that mattered. 'Wow,' he said to her. 'How come you are getting a ride?'

'Anyone can have a ride.'

'Really?'

'Yes, it only costs six-pence.'

'I still don't have any money,' said Jake, and then he pointed to Gorilla Boy's caravan. 'I will see you over there when you are ready.'

Eliza finished her ride and caught up with Jake, having first made sure that there was no one about who might recognise her. 'Riding a real horse is so different to riding the ones on the merry-go-round,' she said, her voice full of excitement.

'That wasn't a real horse,' said Jake. 'Roy Rogers rides a real horse. All the cowboys do.'

'It was a real horse,' insisted Eliza. 'They just make some a bit smaller for kids to ride.'

'Okay, I will just say that it was a real small horse then,' laughed Jake.

'Stop making fun of me. I am going to ask for a pony for Christmas.'

'Where would you keep it?'

'In the back yard.'

'What if it rains. I don't think your dad would let you take it in the house.'

'It could go in the chook house.'

'Have you asked the chooks about that?'

'Jake, you are being silly. What do you want for Christmas?'

'A canoe.'

'But a kid disappeared in a canoe. Would your mum let you have one?'

'Probably not, so I guess I will be getting a surprise.'

Eliza looked up and saw Gorilla Boy walking towards them. 'Hi, Gorilla Boy,' she shouted.

Gorilla Boy stopped, turned, and then began to walk away. Jake and Eliza chased after him.

'Stop,' called Eliza, and Gorilla Boy stopped. 'Didn't you hear us calling you?' she asked.

'Sorry, no hear,' said Gorilla Boy, holding a hand to his ear.

'We are here for our pay,' said Eliza. 'We lost your jar of paste though, so I guess you will have to take some money out for that.'

'Paste never come back,' said Gorilla Boy.

'How come?'

'Police keep it.'

'You knew it was against the law and you didn't tell us,' growled Eliza.

'You didn't ask, but good job. Many posters up.'

'I think a lot of those posters were put up by circus people,' Eliza replied.

'No. Circus people not do. Against law. Always ask others.'

Eliza frowned. 'In that case, you are bad for not telling us.'

'But you here. Not locked up. Circus people get locked up.'

'Well, we would like our pay now please, if you don't mind.'

'No money,' said Gorilla Boy. 'Not enough people come.'

Jake saw the disappointment in Eliza's face and decided to take action. The solution was obvious. He would have to punch Gorilla Boy in the jaw, but there were problems. He had promised his mum that he would not fight, and Gorilla Boy was almost the size of an adult. However, Eliza had been betrayed. 'How would you like a punch in the face?' said Jake.

Gorilla Boy took a step back and replied, 'Let you in free.'

'But Jake and I can't be seen together,' said Eliza.

'No problem. Special seats. No one see.'

Gorilla boy took them to the performers' entrance and walked up to a man who appeared to be standing guard. 'Poster people,' he said to the man, pointing to Jake and Eliza.

The man nodded. 'You did a good job, kids. That is the most posters we have ever managed to put up in the one town.' Then he waved them through.

The circus's seats were wooden planks, mounted in rows on a wooden scaffold. Gorilla Boy took them to the top tier, in a spot that was close to the band. From there, the view was partly obscured by a net that hung from the riggings, but that was a good thing. The net hid them from the audience, and it prevented other people from wanting to sit there. 'Net for trapeze people,' said Gorilla Boy.

'That's okay,' said Eliza. 'This is perfect. Thank you.'

'Good,' was the reply, and then Gorilla Boy left.

Eliza sat there, taking it all in. She had never been to a circus, and this was not the day that she thought she would be going to one for the first time. She was so excited, but she was also puzzled. If the circus people hadn't put up the posters, then who had? She asked Jake for his opinion.

'They must have done it,' he said. 'They just won't admit to it because they know it is against the law.'

19

THE GREATEST SHOW ON EARTH

The kids waited in expectation; Eliza almost overwhelmed by it all. The smell of sawdust, the lights, the colours, the sounds. Even the tent seemed alive, its candy-striped walls gently moving in the afternoon breeze. She had no problem with the hard seats or unfortunate placement of the safety net. Just being there was enough.

The ring master's voice boomed, 'Welcome to the circus, the greatest show on earth!'

'He said this is the greatest show on earth,' gasped Eliza.

'All the circuses say that,' said Jake, who actually had little experience on the subject.

'Shush,' she said. 'I don't want to miss what he is saying.' Then she clapped without realising it, when a musician in a gold uniform heralded the opening on a trumpet.

The show began with a trio of Fox Terriers dressed in tutus, jumping through hoops, and walking on their hind legs. *I could teach Timmy to do that,* thought Jake, but he doubted that Timmy would ever wear a tutu.

Then entered the bareback riders, standing on their prancing ponies. The audience watched as they did circuits of the arena, performing gymnastics upon their white steeds. Then the ring master called for a volunteer. 'You will be attached to a safety rope,' he announced. 'See if you can stand on one of our magnificent chargers without falling off.'

'Go on, Jake, have a go,' said Eliza.

'I don't trust circus people,' said Jake.

Several volunteers raced forward, and one was chosen. To Jake's surprise, Boof was the lucky volunteer. A safety rope dropped from above, then one end of it was attached to a harness that was strapped around Boof's waist. A clown held the other. *Don't trust them, Boof,* thought Jake.

Boof was helped onto a pony, where he stood for a brief moment of glory before the pony moved off. To the amazement of all, Boof stayed on his mount for almost a full circuit before losing balance. Fortunately, the clown came to his rescue and heaved on the safety rope. Boof was hoisted into the air, then he circled the arena in Peter Pan style, just out of reach of other clowns who were trying to catch him.

Darn, thought Jake. *I wish I had volunteered. That looks like fun.*

A clown grabbed Boof by the shorts, and off they came. A pantsless Boof was now circling the arena.

Lucky he remembered to put on undies, thought Jake, but Eliza could only laugh. 'That is the funniest thing I have ever seen,' she said.

Next to entertain the crowd were the three elephants. They strode into the arena, trunks grasped onto tales, an elephant equivalent of people holding hands. Upon their backs rode girls in bright costumes, all waving to the audience. The elephant's trainer walked beside the lead elephant, goading the massive beast with a hooked rod. The tricks that followed featured an elephant standing on a barrel and another sitting on its butt. These were simple tasks for most creatures but were impressive when performed by an elephant.

After the elephants came the lions, which was the most exciting act of them all. The audience watched as circus hands assemble a meshed enclosure. That mesh was all that would stand between the fearsome cats and those who watched on. With timed precision, the enclosure was put into place whilst clowns did stupid things to distract the audience. Then anticipation grew as the lion's cage was wheeled in. The lion trainer entered the enclosure, dressed in khaki, as if having just come from an African safari. At first, he stood alone, and then the lions joined him. One by one, they entered the enclosure, and he called each by name as it entered, and then ordered it to sit on a designated stool. The lions snarled and menaced with their claws, and the trainer had just a whip and chair with which to defend himself. But he stayed cool, commanding them to jump through hoops, roll on the ground, and stand on their hind legs. Eliza was enthralled. It was all happening so close that she could smell the lions.

The show continued, but the lions were a tough act to follow. There were more clowns, jugglers, acrobats, and a tightrope walker. All were exciting, but even the performers on the flying trapeze could not match the courage of the lion tamer. But then, without warning, came the act Jake most wanted to see. 'Ladies and gentlemen, girls and boys,' announced the ringmaster. 'The circus is proud to bring to you the only gorilla in captivity. Behold, direct from the African jungle, the mighty Kong.'

This can't be happening, thought Jake. *They have forgotten to put up the safety enclosure like they did for the lions.*

The mighty Kong entered the ring, tugging on a chain attached to a collar around his neck. Holding on to the chain was a man dressed as Tarzan. Kong thumped his chest, then bounded onto the coloured boxes that formed the perimeter of the arena. He jumped from box to box, completing the full circle of boxes. All the while, Tarzan held on to his chain.

'I wonder what other tricks he does?' said Eliza, but at that moment bad things began to happen. Kong grabbed the chain between his hands, then pulled at it as if it were a Christmas bonbon. The chain snapped and the gorilla was free.

The audience gasped upon seeing a wild gorilla at large. Eliza grabbed Jake by the arm. 'Keep calm, everyone,' announced the ringmaster. 'Our safety marshal will see that no harm comes to you.'

A clown rushed in carrying an oversized rifle. *I guess that's the electrician guy,* thought Jake, recalling his first encounter with Gorilla Boy.

A red light flashed from somewhere above, and then a siren wailed outside.

Kong scrambled part way up the net that hung in front of Jake and Eliza, while circus hands wheeled his cage into the arena. Its door was swung open, and Tarzan shouted, 'Get down from there, Kong. Get in your cage.'

Kong scrambled down the net but ignored the cage. He rushed at the audience, a woman screamed, Kong seemed confused, so he stopped. A clash of cymbals rang out from the band, so Kong rushed at the offending musician, pushing him aside. Then he scrambled up the terraced seats closest to the band, which was where Jake and Eliza were sitting. He stood in front of them, beating his chest, and Eliza was about to scream. But then she heard a voice. 'It's okay, Missy, it's only me.'

The gorilla had spoken, and the voice was unmistakably that of Gorilla Boy. The circus's awesome gorilla was just a kid in a gorilla suit. *What a rip off*, thought Jake.

But the action was not yet over. Kong bounded down to the cage and slammed the door shut. 'Stop, or I shoot,' yelled the safety marshal.

Are we really meant to believe that a gorilla understands English, thought Jake.

Kong gave the marshal a rude gesture with his finger, then bounded out the performers' entrance. The marshal gave chase, then came a loud gunshot. The audience gasped, then fell silent, listening for more sounds from outside. The ring master strode into the arena. 'All is well, folks,' he announced. 'The gorilla now sleeps. Our safety marshal has tranquilized him with a dart, but he will be awake for tonight's show.'

'At least the lions were real,' said Jake as they left when the show was over.

'You're a harsh judge,' laughed Eliza. 'I thought everything was wonderful.'

Jake agreed. He walked Eliza to the corner of her street, then as they parted, she said, 'Don't forget, the dance class is tomorrow afternoon. I hope to see you there.'

'Okay,' said Jake. 'That means you have to come out in the boat with me.'

'Sounds like an adventure,' Eliza laughed, and then as before, she skipped the rest of the way home.

81

20

THE DANCE CLASS

Jake was one of the first to arrive at the Town Jetty the next morning, and he chose what he thought would be the best fishing spot. He propped his bike beside him, reserving a spot for Boof. In the past, the Town Jetty was the place where Jake felt that he was amongst friends, but thanks to Hoppy, Boof was now the only real friend he had. Hoppy was out to get him, and it had begun on that first day when he had sent Jake to the Old Jetty. Since then, Hoppy had been telling people that Jake was dangerous and probably goes around stabbing people. It appeared that Jake had become a target for Cassidy vengeance due to his close friendship with Ben.

Boof arrived soon after, and Jake made ready to answer the same question Boof asked every morning, namely, 'Are the fish biting?' but Boof had a different question this time. 'Who was the girl sitting next to you at the circus yesterday?'

Jake thought that no one would have seen them hiding behind the safety net, but not so. 'How come you saw me?' he asked.

'I saw everyone when I was flying around on that rope.'

'That was funny,' laughed Jake.

'No, it wasn't,' said Boof. 'Now I know why the clown asked me if I was wearing underpants. I thought it to be a very unusual question at the time.'

'You are lucky your underpants didn't come off with your other pants,' said Jake.

'I think the clown loosened my belt when he put me in the safety harness, because my pants came off so easily,' Boof shrugged, 'but I want to know who the girl was that you were with?'

'Just someone who happened to be sitting there,' said Jake.

'I don't believe you,' was Boof's reply. 'What is her name?'

'I don't know.'

'Yes, you do,' and then Boof began to chant, 'Jug's got a girlfriend.'

'I do not have a girlfriend,' Jake snorted.

A kid fishing close by said, 'Is that the girl I saw with Jug's old fishing gear yesterday? She was coming away from the Old Jetty.'

'It would not have been mine,' growled Jake.

'It was,' insisted the kid. 'The rod had a white tip and white bindings, just like your old one.'

Hoppy was listening with interest, and began to chant, 'Jug uses girl's gear.'

'There is no such thing as girl's gear,' growled Jake. 'Girls use the same gear as boys.'

'I think we should call Jug Girlie in future,' laughed Hoppy.

Hoppy's suggestion might have been taken seriously, had Jake's float not taken a sharp turn at that moment. Jake struck and two huge garfish splashed on his line. 'You kids are wasting time while I am catching double headers,' he laughed.

The challenge was on, and there was no more talk about girlfriends or calling Jake Girlie. Everyone was keen to catch more fish than Jake, but he beat them all, and Hoppy's suggestion went no further. No one wanted to be beaten by a kid called Girlie.

Later that afternoon, Jake prepared himself for another challenge, one about which he had no skills at all. He walked into the Sunday School Hall, which was now a dance studio. He was late, for most of the kids were already there. 'Welcome Jake,' came a familiar voice. It appeared that Miss Brown was their dance teacher. 'Go and sit with the boys,' she said.

The boys were sitting along one side of the hall and the girls the other.

Jake sat on the end of the boy's row and glanced at the kid next to him. It was Ivan.

'G'day whispered Jake,' not expecting a reply.

'G'day.'

It appeared that the enemy was prepared to speak. 'Get any fish on your jetty this morning?' Jake asked.

'Lots.'

'Me too.'

'Why are you here?' said Ivan. 'This is for the kids in the Workers Village. How did you get an invite?'

'Just came. Why, are you going to try and kick me out?'

'No.'

Miss Brown clapped her hands to get attention. 'Today, class, we will learn the fox trot. It is an easy dance for beginners.'

Eliza put up her hand. 'What about the jive, Miss Brown?'

'I won't be teaching you the jive,' said Miss Brown. 'That modern stuff will be out of date before you know it, but people will always do the fox trot.'

Ivan shook his head. 'My sister is always pushing her beak in. She's embarrassing.'

'No, she isn't,' said Jake.

'How would you know?'

Jake had no answer.

Miss Brown put a record on the turntable. 'I want the boys to go over and ask a girl for a dance,' she said.

'I think I will ask your embarrassing sister,' quipped Jake.

'She will probably tread on your toes,' came the reply.

Jake walked over to Eliza, making sure that he reached her first. 'Would you like to dance?' he asked.

'I don't know you,' she said. 'Ask someone else.'

'But I told Ivan I was going to ask you,' Jake whispered, but too late. A kid with a ducktail haircut, red checked shirt, and blue denim jeans, cut in.

'How about a dance, cutie?' he asked.

What a creep, thought Jake. *Kids our age don't call girls cutie. Who does he think he is, James Dean or someone?*

'Okay,' said Eliza, and so the miniature rock star took her by the hand.

Jake looked about for another partner, and fortunately, the girls outnumbered the boys. One still sitting was Susie, and she was becoming anxious. She did not want the embarrassment of being one of the unchosen. 'Hi, Jake,' she said in a sweet voice that was most un-Susie-like.

'Hi, Susie.'

'Want to dance?' she asked.

Jake was in a dilemma, but at least, he would be dancing with a girl he knew, and to refuse would only heighten their frosty relationship. 'Okay,' he said.

The kids formed a circle and watched Miss Brown go through the steps. Then she showed the boys how to hold their partners. Jake frowned and looked at Eliza. Holding your partner was not the sort of dance he thought they would be learning. 'Come on,' said Susie. 'The music is about to start.'

Jake held Susie but it felt weird. Even talking to her was something he always avoided, but having to hold her in his arms was taking things to a whole new level. *I hope this record doesn't play for long,* he thought.

The music began. 'You are starting on the wrong foot,' growled Susie.

'Sorry.'

'Go the other way or people will bump into us.'

'They should watch where they're going,' said Jake.

'But you're the one at fault, and you are making me look silly.'

Jake glanced across to Eliza. She was in the arms of an expert, being dragged around the floor like a rag doll, stumbling to stay in step with her partner's immaculate dance moves. *Mister Cool already knows how to danc*e, thought Jake. *He is only here to show off.*

Jake blundered into the path of Ivan, and Ivan saw his chance. His foot came out, tripping Jake who fell to the floor, and Susie got flattened in the process.

Miss Brown stopped the music. 'Are you alright, Susie?' she asked.

'No, I hurt my knee. Jake pushed me over.' She began to cry.

Everyone stared at Jake, and he felt as if he had turned into a monster. 'I didn't mean to do it,' he said.

'Everyone sit down while I attend to Susie's injury,' said Miss Brown. She brought out the first aid kit, but the only thing needed was a handkerchief for Susie to blow her nose. 'Are you ready to start dancing again, Susie?' asked Miss Brown.

'No. My knee still hurts.'

'You will have to choose another partner,' Jake was told. Miss Brown turned to the girls without partners. 'Who would like to dance with Jake?' she asked, but there were no volunteers.

Jake's first dancing experience was going from bad to worse. No one wanted to dance with him. Again, he was the outsider, rejected by all. He was only there to please Eliza, but she did not need him. She was in the capable arms of a dancing expert.

Then Eliza put up her hand. 'I will dance with Jake,' she said. 'My partner, Donald, is such a good dancer. He deserves to be dancing with someone better than me.'

'Who would like to dance with Donald?' asked Miss Brown, and all the girls put up their hand.

The fox trot resumed, and Jake was no longer bothered if he got some of the steps wrong, because Eliza was getting them wrong too. 'Sorry, what happened,' she said. 'I didn't want to dance with Donald, and I saw what Ivan did to you.'

'So, you don't like boys who are good dancers?'

'Not necessarily, but I hated him from the moment he called me cutie.'

Jake felt happier for having been rescued by Eliza. 'If I ever see that kid again, I will call him Donald Duck,' he laughed.

Eliza giggled.

It was just before the dance class ended that Eliza told Jake that she would have to go straight home. 'Meet me under the Jetty at three tomorrow,' said Jake.

'What if I can't make it?'

'Then try again the next day.'

'But what if that doesn't work either?'

'We will just have to keep trying.'

'Okay.'

Jake realised that they needed a better way to stay in contact, which was something he would have to think about.

21

IN TROUBLE WITH DAD

Jake went for a bike ride around the district, annoyed that he was doing it alone because he could not be seen with Eliza. He arrived home just in time to see Biggles leaving his house once more.

'Jake, you are in real trouble with the law now,' said his mum.

'How come?'

'Do you know a girl called Susie?'

'Yes.'

'And did you deliberately push her onto the floor of the church hall today?'

'No.'

'Officer Biggs said you did.'

'Someone tripped me, and I accidently pushed her as I fell, but how come it's a police matter?'

'Susie is Councillor Cassidy's niece, and the councillor has made an official complaint. Officer Biggs definitely has you in his sights and says he is going to get you for what you did to Gerald's bike.'

'I didn't touch Hoppy's bike.'

'I know,' said his mum, 'but how come you and Susie were at the church hall?'

'I was learning to dance.'

'WHAT!' came a voice from the next room. Jake's dad had been listening and he came storming in. 'The dance classes the church puts on are for the kids in the Workers Village, and they are not the type of kids your mother and I want you to mix with, especially the girls. That is why we send you to college.'

'But Susie goes to the dance class, and she doesn't live in the Workers Village, so other kids can go there as well,' Jake argued.

His dad took a deep breath. 'No self-respecting parent in this town allows their kids to mix with the Workers Village kids. Half their parents can't even speak our language, and why are you learning to dance anyway? At your age, I was playing football and cricket with the boys. Only the sissies were learning to dance.'

'But you know how to dance now,' said Jake.

'I learnt when I was much older than you. Girls just distract a young man's attention at a time when he has far more important things to focus on.'

Jake had hoped to invite Eliza to his house, but that was now out of the question. He was facing the worst situation a kid can face, for he had always turned to his parents to fix a problem, but what does he do when the problem is his parents? He would have to ask Ben for advice.

Next day, Jake explained the situation to Ben, who was sympathetic. 'Eliza is a nice girl who any dad would be proud to have as a daughter,' he said, 'but she faces the same problem that all the newcomers face. Your dad is old school, a descendant of our first settlers, and he resents people who come here from a foreign land. Then there are others, like Councilor Cassidy, who use their power to exploit the new arrivals. Everyone deserves a fair go, and it will be up to your generation to bring our divided community together.' But then Ben had good news. 'Guess what?' he said.

'What?' asked Jake.

'I have done something I have been trying to do for years.'

'You almost broke the land speed record in your car,' Jake laughed.

'No.'

'You got your wife to mow the lawn.'

'No.'

'You've worked out a way to put Councillor Cassidy's hardware store out of business.'

'You are very close,' said Ben. 'I have a rich friend who has been coming here since he was a boy, just like you. When I told him what Cassidy was doing, he decided to help, and I now have an unlimited supply of Ferris wheel tickets.'

'That's fantastic,' exclaimed Jake. 'I can't wait to tell the kids, but how is that going to put your opposition out of business?'

'Every customer who buys something from my shop gets a free Ferris wheel ticket from now on,' Ben laughed.

'But won't he just start giving out free merry-go-round tickets?'

'Which would you rather have, a ride on a merry-go-round or a ride on a Ferris wheel?'

'The Ferris wheel.'

'Precisely. The customers are going to flock in here.'

Then Ben gave Jake a strip of Ferris wheel tickets. 'Take these and give them to your friends,' he said. 'They can choose between your tickets or Hoppy's merry-go-round. My guess is that Hoppy will have lost most of his so-called friends by the end of the holidays.'

'Hoppy doesn't have any real friends,' said Jake. 'Kids just pretend to like him because he has stuff that other kids don't.'

Jake left Ben's shop with a pocket full of tickets and a promise of more once they were gone. For once, he felt that his days of being the outsider might be over. However, he had no idea how his generation could ever fix the things that Ben thought were wrong.

22

A SECRET CODE

It was too early to meet Eliza under the jetty, but Jake did not want to go home. He went to the beach, the place that could always lift his spirits. To him, that narrow strip of sand between land and sea, held a magic he could never explain. He sat on the warning seat, thinking about all that Ben had said that morning. Ben was in a struggle with a powerful enemy, but he had found a friend to help him fight back. Ben had also said that the newcomers had similar problems, like Jake's dad resenting Eliza. Jake stared out to sea, thinking about things from Eliza's viewpoint. Like Ben, she also needed a friend to help her fight back, and he was going to be that friend. His dad did not have the right to stop him.

Bottles came by and sat on the seat beside him.

'Ug, Bottles,' said Jake. 'Sorry I'm sitting on your seat.'

'Ug,' grunted Bottles, and then he pointed towards the Old Jetty, waving his hands, gesturing for Jake to go there.

'You want me to go to the Old Jetty?' queried Jake.

'Ug,' Bottles nodded.

'But what's there?'

Bottles leant forward and wrote in the sand, *Girl*.

'There is a girl at the Old Jetty?' queried Jake.

Bottles nodded and waved his hands once more, again gesturing Jake to go.

Jake bid Bottles farewell and headed for the Old Jetty, hid his bike in the usual spot, then made his way along the seawall. To his surprise, Eliza was already there. She was lying on the beach, not far from the jetty, and was reading a book. When she saw Jake sneak into their secret meeting place, she joined him. 'You are early,' she said. 'How did you know that I would be here already?'

'Bottles told me.'

91

'Why would Bottles do that? He doesn't even know we are friends.'

'Yes, he does. He saw us putting up a circus poster at the church.'

'That's right, I remember now,' recalled Eliza. 'He was the one who tore it down. I don't think he likes us, so why would he tell you I was here and how did he know that this is where we meet?'

'I don't know,' said Jake, 'but Bottles seems to notice things that other people don't.' Then he reached into his pocket. 'Guess what these are?' he said.

'No idea. Where did you find them?'

'They are free Ferris wheel tickets. Ben gave them to me. We can have as many rides as we like.'

'Where did Ben find them?'

'Ben didn't find them. He is a friend of the Ferris wheel's owner and can get as many free tickets as he wants.'

'That sounds exciting,' said Eliza. 'I have never been on a Ferris wheel, but I am not sure what time I can meet you tomorrow.'

'Not a problem,' said Jake. 'I have invented a secret code. If ever I want to see you, I will ride past your house making a special noise. Then I will wait on the corner and watch for you to come out. If you throw a ball into the air once, I will go to the jetty and wait. If you throw it up twice, I will come past again in half an hour. Then, for every extra time you throw it up, I will add another half hour.'

'That sounds very complicated,' said Eliza.'

'Meeting codes have to be complicated, or people will work them out,' said Jake.

'What if I want to see you?' she asked.

'I will tell you where I live, and you can do the same at my place.'

'But what sort of special noise can I make?'

'That's easy,' said Jake. He pulled a clothes' peg and a square of cardboard from his back pocket. 'Use this peg to clamp the cardboard on to the back fork of your bike. When you push the cardboard into the spokes, it makes a noise like a motorbike, and the faster you ride, the better it sounds.'

'I am not making my bike sound like a motorbike,' said Eliza. 'That would be embarrassing.'

'But kids do it all the time.'

'No. Boys do it all the time, but girls think it's silly. I need a better suggestion.'

How could that be silly? thought Jake. The motorbike sound was one of the best things ever invented for a bike, and it cost nothing to install. He thought some more. *What sort of sound could a girl make without being embarrassed.* Then he came up with an idea, and it was so clever, that only a genius would think of it. 'Just rattle my front gate,' he said.

'But you probably won't hear that,' said Eliza.

'No, but Timmy will. He goes mad when he hears the slightest rattle of the front gate. The whole district hears him.' Then Jake described his house. 'You will find it easy,' he said. 'It is the only house in the street that has a red tiled roof, a brick front fence, and a front lawn surrounded by rose bushes. I think it is the best-looking house in the street.'

'Does it have a number on the letter box?' asked Eliza.

'Yes, it has the number 12.'

'Good, I will just look for the number 12,' she laughed. 'Would you like me to describe my house?'

'Okay.'

Eliza smiled. 'Well, all the houses in our street look the same, but our house has a shiny new tap next to the letterbox. Dad put it there last week to make it easier for him to water the vegetables he has growing in the front yard.'

'Isn't your dad afraid that people will pinch his vegetables?' asked Jake.

'No, because most of the people in our street grow vegetables out the front and we share. Perhaps your dad should be growing vegetables, rather than roses.'

'My dad doesn't have to grow vegetables,' said Jake. 'Dad is a vegetable wholesaler at the market, and once the market is over for the morning, he delivers vegetables in his van.'

'That means our dads are both drivers,' exclaimed Eliza. 'My dad was an electronics engineer, and he worked on radar systems during the war, but he drives a garbage truck these days. It is the only job he has been able to get since our family arrived in Australia. But I guess that means our dads have a lot in common, because they both drive for a living.'

'I don't think my dad would see it that way,' said Jake, 'because he has banned me from seeing you.'

'Why?'

'I don't know. Ben says he is old school and needs to change.'

'How come you are here seeing me then?' she smiled.

'Because Dad is wrong, and friends must stick together,' said Jake, 'but I have to make sure that he does not find out about you.'

'That sounds silly.'

Jake agreed.

When it came time to leave that day, Jake decided to test his secret code, so he gave Eliza a few minutes head start and then headed for her street.

The cardboard roared in his spokes. *How could anyone find that noise embarrassing,* he thought. He arrived at Eliza's corner, and for the first time, he noticed that the houses were all the same, just as she had said. Had it not been for their windows and doors, they could have been mistaken for a row of large boxes. However, the third house from the corner did have a shiny tap at the front.

Jake rode past the house with the shiny tap, then returned to the corner. He watched Eliza come out of the house and begin bouncing a ball on the ground, but bouncing the ball was not part of the code. He left, confused, wondering how it was that Eliza had failed to grasp the simple concept of the code he had invented.

23

THE FERRIS WHEEL

Jake's next test of his secret code was to come the next day, which was when he hoped Eliza and he would go riding on the Ferris wheel. The plan was that once she had finished her jobs, she would go to his place and rattle the front gate. The rest would be up to Timmy.

Jake was lying on the lounge room floor, listening to the wireless. The top ten hits were playing, and he wanted to know what would be number one that week, but the wireless was old, and static was spoiling much of his enjoyment. The family needed to replace it, but his dad was not prepared to buy a new one because they were saving to buy a TV.

Jake's listening was interrupted by an outburst of barking. The code was working. *Eliza will be waiting at the end of the street,* he thought. He grabbed a tennis ball and ran outside, but it was just Timmy barking at Mrs. Bradley's cat. 'Stop barking,' growled Jake.

He went back inside and listened to the rest of the Top Ten, but not another bark did Timmy make. *Perhaps Eliza isn't coming,* he thought. He became restless, and whenever that happened, his tummy would give him a message. He needed a snack, so he went looking for his mum, the source of all things edible, and he found her weeding the front garden. 'A strange thing just happened,' she said.

'What?' asked Jake.

'A girl came by a little while ago and rattled our front gate.'

'Really. Did Timmy bark?'

'No. He just wagged his tail, but she was a lovely girl. We had a nice chat, and now she seems to be waiting for someone down at the corner. I can just see her yellow hat through the bushes.'

Jake's ingenious code had been foiled by the incompetence of a dog, but all was not lost. He had the ball with him, and he held it out. A single throw into the air would tell Eliza that he was on his way.

A Ball! thought Timmy, and the agile canine snatched it from Jake's hand.

'Give it back,' Jake yelled, but Timmy bolted. He chased the fugitive dog into the back yard, where Timmy lost the ball under the rainwater tank, but Jake did not see where it went. 'Timmy, find the ball,' he yelled, but Timmy just squatted on the ground.

Jake's code had flaws, leaving its inventor with no choice other than to hop on his bike and see if Eliza was still waiting.

'I will be home in time for tea,' he said to his mum as he left.

'Bye, Sweetie. Let me know if that girl is still down there. She makes me curious.'

Jake raced to the corner where Eliza was waiting. 'Hi, Jake, your mum seems nice,' she said.

'She is,' said Jake, 'but what did you talk about?'

'Vegetables mainly.'

'Oh.'

'But what happened to our secret code?' asked Eliza.

'Timmy let the team down.'

'But you were supposed to throw a ball in the air.'

'I couldn't. Timmy ran away with it.'

Eliza laughed. 'That's okay,' she said. 'I've worked out a new code for your place next time.'

'What?'

'I am just going to knock on your door and show your mum one of dad's great tomatoes.'

'That will only work once,' said Jake.

'No, because dad grows all kinds of things and so do the neighbours. I can bring something different every day.'

'But the code doesn't work at your place either,' said Jake. 'Why did you bounce the ball on the ground yesterday? Bouncing the ball is not in the code.'

'I had to make a code up because we don't have one for *see you tomorrow*.'

'We have the every half hour ball toss code,' said Jake.

'Jake, I was not seeing you for twenty-four-hours, and I am not throwing a ball up forty-eight times. Bouncing the ball is my new code. It means, I will see you tomorrow.'

'Okay,' said Jake. 'I will leave you in charge of the code from now on, and sorry for making you wait.'

They parked their bikes close to the Ferris wheel and joined the queue for the next ride. Eliza counted the patrons ahead, working out which chair would be theirs. 'I think we are getting the yellow one,' she said. 'That has to be lucky.'

Eliza was enjoying the moment. Her summer holiday was becoming far more exciting than expected. She had been to the pictures, a circus, and was now about to have her first ride on a Ferris wheel.

They watched the yellow chair descend, its occupants rocking it back and forth, getting the last bit of enjoyment for their money. 'Don't you dare rock the chair like that,' said Eliza. 'Just being up so high will be scary enough for me.'

The yellow chair stopped at the boarding platform and its occupants got out. 'Is it scary?' Eliza asked them.

'Only if you rock the chair,' said the girl, and then she pointed to her boyfriend. 'I kept telling him to stop doing it, but he wouldn't.'

The kids took their place and were soon enjoying one of the Ferris wheel's special features. Unlike a merry-go-round, a Ferris wheel ride does not begin at once. Eliza found how the excitement builds as each chair takes its turn at the boarding platform, for their chair would be raised a little higher each time. Finally, the yellow chair was at the highest point of the ride. 'I can see Ben's shop from here,' she said.

'I thought you might be afraid of heights,' Jake replied.

'I've changed my mind about that,' said Eliza. 'What is there to be afraid of?'

Jake laughed. 'This chair is attached to the Ferris wheel with bolts, and if one comes out, the chair might go crashing to the ground.'

'Actually, that bolt behind your head does look a bit loose,' giggled Eliza.

Jake spun around to inspect the suspect bolt. 'Which one?' he asked.

'Just kidding,' she said, and then she giggled some more.

The wheel began to turn full circle, and Eliza counted each turn as they reached the top. 'I wonder how many times it goes around,' she said.

'Doesn't matter,' said Jake. 'I have enough tickets to keep us riding all afternoon.'

'Good.' she said, and then she added, 'Hang on. I am going to try something.'

Eliza began to rock the chair. 'This feels fun,' she said. 'I am going to do this all the way around. I want to see if it is scarier going up or coming down.'

'I thought you didn't want to rock the chair,' said Jake.

'I've changed my mind about that as well.'

'But are you sure that bolt you talked about isn't loose?' Jake asked.

'I don't think so,' she said. 'If it were loose, rocking this chair would probably make it fall out.'

After four turns, the ride was over, but Eliza was not over with the rides. 'Give the man two more tickets,' she said. 'I want to go again.'

The second ride began with Eliza rocking the chair once more, but this time a couple on the opposite side of the wheel copied what they were doing. 'They are doing bigger rocks than us,' said Eliza. 'Come on, Jake, help me.'

Jake was discovering that Eliza was not only a dare devil; she was competitive as well. 'We might get into trouble if we rock too hard,' he said.

'Jake, there are no loose bolts and I know we can rock this chair better than them.'

'Why?'

'Because it's yellow.'

Jake had no choice. Being a Ferris wheel wimp was no way to impress a girl. He summoned up his courage and they soon had the chair at its full rocking potential. Then the ride was over.

'Going again?' asked the attendant.

'No thank you,' said Eliza. 'We will come back later.'

Jake was surprised by her decision. 'I thought you would want to go again,' he said.

'Later. I feel like some fairy floss now.'

'But I haven't got any money.'

'That's okay,' said Eliza. 'I still have one and sixpence left over from the two shillings I found at the pictures. I can shout you.'

24

BOOF'S WARNING

Eliza stood at the fairy floss stall, watching a cup of pink sugar being spun into thousands of strands of sweet fairy floss. Meanwhile, Jake stood some distance away, taking care that they were not seen together. Riding the Ferris wheel was a risk worth taking, but just standing at the fairy floss stall was not. Then a voice came from the shooting gallery. 'Hey, Jug, come over here while I finish my shots.' It appeared that Jake's caution had been for good reason, for Boof was standing at the shooting gallery, firing slugs at a passing parade of tin ducks. Jake ignored him.

Eliza came back and handed Jake a bag of fairy floss. 'Enjoy,' she said.

'Thank you,' said Jake, and then he added, 'let's get out of here and go for a bike ride.'

But Boof shouted again. 'Hey, Jug, what's new?'

'Is that kid shouting at you?' asked Eliza. 'He looks like the underpants kid from the circus.'

'He is, and we need to avoid him,' said Jake, but the game was over.

Boof came running up. 'Hi, Jug, didn't you hear me?' he asked.

'Hi, Boof. I thought you were someone else.'

'I didn't know you had a sister,' said Boof.

'Eliza isn't my sister.'

'I was right then,' Boof said with glee. 'You do have a girlfriend.'

'Eliza is just an ordinary friend, and you can't tell anyone about her,' said Jake.

'Why?'

'Because her brother is the leader of the Old Jetty Gang, and my dad doesn't want me mixing with girls.'

'Did your dad give a reason?'

'Sort of. Dad says girls are a distraction to boys at a time when they need to be thinking about their future careers.'

'That sounds boring,' laughed Boof. 'What do you think of it all?' he asked Eliza.

'I would like you to keep our secret please,' she replied. 'There could be real trouble if my brother finds out that I am friends with a Town Jetty kid.'

'Okay,' said Boof, 'but I have to warn you, Jake is a wanted man.'

'How come?'

Boof became serious and told how Councillor Cassidy had stepped up his campaign against Ben and Jake. There was now a new reward poster in his shop window, regarding the attempted murder of his son.

'Calling it attempted murder is stupid,' said Jake.

'It is worse than that,' said Boof, 'because the new poster has your picture on it and words that read, *This Boy is a Suspect*.'

'Did you do it?' Eliza asked Jake.

'No, but if I ever find the kid who did, I will give him a bunch of Ferris wheel tickets,' Jake laughed.

'When did messing with a bike become an attempted murder case?' asked Eliza.

'It depends on whose bike you mess with,' said Boof. 'Hoppy is a protected species around here.'

Jake reached into his pocket. 'Here, Boof, have some Ferris wheel tickets, but you can't tell anyone about Eliza.'

Boof's eyes popped open. 'How many have you got?'

'As many as I want,' said Jake. 'Ben has started giving them to me to hand out to my friends.'

'Hoppy won't be happy about that,' laughed Boof. 'You could become the new leader of the Town Jetty Gang.'

'His dad won't be happy either,' laughed Jake, 'and I think that is part of Ben's plan.'

Boof could see that the Ferris wheel was about to begin another ride. 'I'm off to grab a seat,' he said, gleefully waving his tickets in the air.

'Why did he call you Jug?' asked Eliza once Boof had gone.

'My real name is Jake Jones, so he calls me Jughead Jones like in the Archie comics.'

'So, you call him Boof, like in the Boof Head comics.'

'That's right.'

'I think calling people awful names is silly,' said Eliza.

'Why? I heard someone call you Doolittle,' laughed Jake. 'Does that mean you don't do very much?'

'Doolittle is not an awful name,' Eliza frowned. 'My dad calls me Doolittle, after Eliza Doolittle in the stage play, Pygmalion.'

'How come your dad knows about an English play?'

'Dad loves the arts and speaks several languages,' said Eliza.

'I didn't think garbage truck drivers were that well educated,' Jake replied.

'My dad is a very clever man,' Eliza growled. 'He was a chess champion in his younger days, and lately, he has been teaching me to play.'

'We should have a game then,' said Jake.

'I don't want to.'

'Why, is it because I have a chess scholarship and you know I will win?'

'No, it is because I hate to lose.'

'That means the same thing.'

'It can actually mean something quite different,' she said.

Jake was puzzled. 'Don't worry about it,' he laughed. 'Chess is just a fun game. It doesn't matter who wins. I was thinking about taking the boat out tomorrow, but we could have a game of chess the day after. Are you still going to come out in the boat with me?'

'I would love to,' said Eliza.

'What about the chess challenge?'

'Maybe.'

The Ferris wheel had revealed Eliza's competitive spirit, but that probably meant she was a bad loser. *I must remember to always be humble in victory,* thought Jake.

The kids spent the rest of the afternoon riding the Ferris wheel and enjoying a seagull's view of the foreshore. Then it came time to go. 'I will launch by the warning seat at ten tomorrow morning,' said Jake, 'and you don't have to bring any fishing gear.'

'Okay. I will bring lunch then.'

'Yum. That sounds good,' Jake replied.

25

GIRL OVERBOARD

Jake's dad owned a small rowboat that could be wheeled to the beach, and Jake was allowed to take it out on his own. Next morning, he pushed it along the road with Timmy as his sidekick. Timmy was useless in the pushing department, but he considered himself an important part of the team because he cleared their path of stray cats.

They arrived at the warning seat where Eliza was waiting with a picnic basket in her hand. 'Someone has left flowers on the warning seat,' she said.

'Flowers get left there every year,' said Jake. 'It happens on the anniversary of the boy's disappearance.'

'You mean today is the same day as when the boy got eaten by a shark?'

'Yes, and I guess that man-eater has probably grown since then.'

'I have heard that sharks come back to the same place every year,' said Eliza.

'You will be safe,' said Jake. 'Dad and I go fishing off here all the time.'

The boat was launched, and everyone climbed on board. Timmy sat on the bow, wagging his tail, while Jake sat in the middle, pulling on the oars. Eliza sat at the stern, looking over the side, surveying the seabed as they passed over it. The sea was calm, and the water clear. It was a perfect day for boating.

Jake anchored the boat about half a mile from shore then hung a burley box over the back. 'Now we have to wait for the burley to attract the fish,' he said.

Unfortunately, the fish seemed to have other things to do that morning. Eliza opened the picnic basket. 'Have a scone,' she said. 'I made them myself.' She cut a scone in half and buttered it with butter she had brought with her in a small jar. 'Sorry that I only have butter to put on them.'

'That's okay,' said Jake. 'I love buttered scones.'

Jake took a bite, but the scones seemed firm, unlike the soft scones that his mum made. 'When did you bake these?' he asked.

'Last night. I made them especially for us.'

'Oh.'

'Well, do you like them?'

There are times in life when you just have to lie, and this was one of them. She was smiling at him, expecting a positive answer, and they were in a tiny boat. He gave the only answer possible when escape was not an option. 'Yes, they are very nice,' he said.

'Good, have another. I've made plenty, so you can take some home and have them tonight as well.'

'Thanks.'

Jake offered a scone to Timmy, but it was ignored. Timmy had spied a large squid lurking just beyond the stern. He growled, and then Jake saw the squid as well. Jake reached into his tackle box and pulled out a squid jag and potato. 'What is the potato for?' asked Eliza, as she put her scones back into the picnic basket.

'It's squid bait,' said Jake. 'I am going to carve it into the shape of a fish and put it on my squid jag.'

'But squid don't eat potatoes.'

'Squid attack anything that looks like a fish,' Jake explained.'

Jake carved the potato and put it on the jag.

'That looks nothing like a fish,' Eliza laughed.

'That is because you are not a squid,' said Jake. He threw the jag over the back and the squid grabbed it without hesitation.

Eliza was surprised. 'That is the stupidest creature I have ever seen,' she said.

The line tugged in the hands of the excited squidder and Timmy began to bark. But then a cloud of ink appeared in the water and Eliza sensed danger. She scrambled to the bow for safety.

Jake lifted the ill-fated squid aboard, but in a flash, Timmy grabbed it. He ripped it off the jag and now everyone was in danger. Squid are notorious squirters of ink when being landed, a situation best controlled by pointing the squid in a direction of minimum harm, but Timmy had no knowledge of such things. The squid let fly and Jake's face was the unfortunate recipient of slimy squid ink. He shut his eyes and closed his mouth but could do nothing about his nostrils.

Jake had squid ink on his face, in his hair, in his eyebrows, but worst of all, up his nose. It was a situation that called for sympathy, but all he could hear was laughter coming from the front of the boat. 'We are lucky we didn't get any on our clothes,' laughed Eliza. 'Even Timmy dodged it all.'

Jake wiped his face with a rag, which gave Timmy an opportunity to maul Jake's catch, but then he stopped. He stood rigid, glaring at something he had seen not far from the boat.

'What is Timmy looking at?' asked Eliza, but Jake was too busy blowing squid ink out of his nose.

Dark thoughts came to Eliza. They were probably on the exact spot where a boy had been eaten by a monster shark, and it happened on that very day some years before. Sharks were known to return to the same place every year, and Timmy had just seen something in the water. Eliza saw the fur bristle on Timmy's neck, and then a large fin appeared a few feet from the boat. She screamed and Timmy barked, but by the time Jake had stopped blowing his nose, the fin was gone. 'Did you see that?' yelled Eliza.

'Did I see what?'

'There is a huge shark circling us and this boat is so tiny.'

Timmy looked over the other side and began to bark even louder.

'Stop barking, Timmy,' said Eliza. 'You are attracting sharks.'

Jake had to put on a brave face. He had often fished with his dad on that spot, and they had never seen a shark, but the concerns of his crew were making him nervous. 'It will soon be a bit too windy to be out here,' he said. 'I think we should go in.'

'Good idea,' said Eliza. 'I will pull up the anchor.'

Jake had just begun to row when he saw a swirl in the water. A dolphin's fin broke the surface and Timmy barked once more.

'It is just a dolphin,' said Jake, but Eliza was not convinced.

'Row faster,' she said.

Jake rowed on, but then he saw another problem ahead. He had hoped to be returning to a deserted beach, but people were gathered at the warning seat. He guessed they had come to remember the lost boy, but he did not want to be seen with Eliza. 'I will have to drop you off further along the beach,' he said.

'You can't go towards the Old Jetty,' said Eliza. 'I can see Ivan and his friends playing soccer on the sand.'

'But I can't go the other way either,' said Jake. 'Hoppy and some of the others are playing golf on that part of the beach. You will have to swim ashore on your own.'

'What about the shark?'

'It was a dolphin.'

'Timmy thinks it was a shark.'

'Timmy doesn't know the difference.'

'But I will get my clothes wet.'

'Got any better ideas?'

'No, but this is the worst boat trip I have ever had.'

It was then that Timmy spotted a flock of seagulls on the beach. He jumped over the side, having no concerns about sharks or getting his fur wet. His only thought was to ruin the seagulls' day.

Eliza decided to follow, and she jumped into neck deep water. Then she swam faster than she had ever swum before, and luckily, no shark attack occurred, nor did her brother see his sodden sister appear from out of the ocean.

Jake arrived home, disappointed that the day had been such a failure, but more bad things were about to happen. The family's one and only wireless was in the street, sitting next to the rubbish bin. It meant one of two things. The family either had a new wireless, or they now had no wireless at all. Jake went inside and found the worst of the two options to be correct. It appeared that his dad had given the wireless a thump that morning, trying to stop the static, which he had succeeded in doing, but now the wireless made no noise at all. The unfortunate wireless had then gone to the electrical shop for repairs, but it could not be revived.

Then came more bad news. Officer Biggs had called again. It appeared that Councillor Cassidy had found a witness who had seen Jake near Hoppy's bike at the time of the great, unsolved crime, but he was keeping the name of the witness under wraps. Jake's mum was now worried because she had given Jake a false alibi, but she was not prepared to change it, despite what the officer had just told her.

26

THE CHESS CHALLENGE

Jake had a sleepless night, for nothing was going right for him, and Eliza was now on the list of people he had upset. Even his fishing the next morning could not ease his troubled mind. His thoughts were only about Eliza. He had promised her a nice day in the boat, but the day had been a disaster. All he could think about, was her trudging home, soaked to the skin. How angry she would have been because he had made her swim ashore. He looked towards the Old Jetty, knowing she would be there, hoping that she could sense the thoughts he was sending across the water. *Sorry,* he was thinking.

However, not everything was going wrong for him that morning, because for once in his life, he no longer felt like an outsider. He had arrived with a pocket full of Ferris wheel tickets and was now the most popular kid on the jetty. Everyone was offered a free ride and only Hoppy refused. 'I prefer to go on the merry-go-round,' he said, but no one shared his opinion.

Jake left the jetty hoping that most would now ignore Hoppy's lies about him, but he was still in trouble with Eliza. He thought about the chess challenge, and how she had said that she did not like to lose. If they played and he let her win, she might forgive him for their shambolic boating adventure. His pride would take a dent, for he would be losing to a novice, but Eliza's friendship was worth the humiliation.

It was only when he went to put his chess set into Eliza's picnic basket, which she had left in the boat the day before, that he discovered the scones. He had forgotten all about them. *Oh no,* he thought. *I can't throw them away. Perhaps they can be toasted.*

He cut two scones in half and popped them into the toaster, and the aroma was soon wafting through the house. His mum came into the kitchen. 'That smells nice, Sweetie. What are you toasting for lunch?'

'Scones.'

'Who gave you scones?'

'A friend.'

'Which friend?'

'You wouldn't know her.'

'It's a girl then.'

Eliza's scones had become Jake's downfall. They had led to unexpected questioning, causing him to accidentally reveal that he was flaunting his dad's *No Girls Rule,* but fortunately, it was his mum doing the asking, his dad was at work.

'Yes, she is a girl,' confessed Jake, 'but I don't know her that well.'

'She must be a nice girl though,' said his mum. 'Probably like the nice girl I was talking to at the gate the other day.' Jake saw his mum look away, but he could tell that she was hiding a smile. 'I don't think we should tell your dad about the scones,' she said.

Jake and his mum shared the two toasted scones and then toasted two more. They were delicious, their overnight stay in the picnic basket had given them a perfect level of staleness for toasting. 'You will have to ask your friend for the recipe,' said his mum.

Jake finished a third helping and headed out the door, carrying the picnic basket. But as he went to hop on his bike, he saw the wireless still sitting on the footpath, waiting to be picked up by the garbage truck. His source of entertainment for so many years was now condemned to spend the rest of eternity in the dump. Then an idea came to him. Perhaps there was someone who could save it. He put the condemned item under his arm and set off on his bike.

Now, some might think that riding a bike with a wireless under one arm while hanging a picnic basket from the handlebars, was dangerous, but Jake considered himself to be a bike riding expert. However, Biggles was one who thought otherwise, and he drew his motorbike alongside the offending cyclist. 'Pull over,' he commanded.

What followed, was another lecture from Biggles. 'You are breaking the law again, Jake Jones. I have to keep my eye on you, and you should be warned, that it is only a matter of time before you will be charged for what you did to Gerald's bike.'

'I was nowhere near Gerald's bike that morning,' protested Jake, 'so stop telling my mum that someone said they saw me there. It is making her upset.'

'I am only doing my job,' said Biggles, 'which includes making sure that you don't have an accident, so get off your bike and walk with those things you are carrying.'

Jake arrived at the Old Jetty having walked the rest of the way. 'You're a bit late,' said Eliza.

'Biggles made me walk,' Jake replied, 'and I am sorry about what happened yesterday.' He looked at her, and for the first time, he expected to see her angry face and hear her angry voice. He guessed her angry voice would be cold, possibly loud, a voice that would strip all feeling of joy from his heart.

'That's okay,' she said. 'If Ivan wasn't so stupid, you could have taken me ashore without a problem.'

Her voice was the same as always, and in that moment, Jake realised that her way of speaking was one of the things that made him feel good.

'Why do you have a wireless with you?' she asked.

'It's broken, but I was hoping your dad could fix it. You said he was an electronics engineer.'

'I will ask him,' said Eliza. 'Did you eat all the scones?'

'I toasted them.'

'But you don't toast fresh scones. You only toast scones that have gone stale. You hate my scones, don't you?'

'Your scones were delicious,' said Jake. 'Mum even wants the recipe.'

'Really?'

'Yes, really.'

Eliza smiled. 'I am not sure I can give her one. I started with a recipe, but the mixture seemed wrong, so I just kept putting stuff in.'

'Would you like a game of chess?' asked Jake.

'I warned you that I don't like to lose,' said Eliza.

'Warning noted,' Jake laughed, then he produced the chess set from the basket and set up the pieces.

'Okay, but just remember that this is your idea,' she said.

The kids sprawled on the sand with the game between them. 'You go first,' said Jake, 'because your side is white.'

But just as the game was about to start, they had an unexpected visitor. Bottles appeared, and he seemed interested in what they were doing. Jake had suspected that Bottles knew about their secret meeting place, because he had told him about Eliza being there a couple of days before.

'Hi, Bottles,' they both said.

'Ug,' he replied, and then he sat down on their seaweed wall, converting it into a comfortable lounge.

'Do you want to watch us play?' Jake asked.

Bottles gave a thumbs up.

The game began, and Jake no longer felt the need to let Eliza win, because she had forgiven him for their offshore disaster. He played with earnest, giving careful thought to every move, while Eliza seemed carefree. Then Eliza appeared to make an obvious mistake. Jake smiled, for his bishop was about to make an important kill, but just as he went to move the chosen assassin, Bottles coughed. They both looked up at Bottles who was shaking his head.

Jake returned to the game and moved his bishop, then Eliza moved her castle. 'Check mate,' she said. The game was over, and Jake had lost.

'Darn,' said Jake. 'I missed seeing that because Bottles put me off. Let's go again. This time I will start.' He glared at Bottles, who responded with a shrug.

The following game took a little longer because Jake started with the advantage. He tried the only set play he knew, but Eliza was aware of it. Then he set a new trap, intending to sacrifice a rook as bait. However, as he went to move the rook, Bottles gave a grunt. Once again, Bottles was shaking his head, but Jake was not to be put off for a second time. Bottles was clearly unaware that the rook was being sacrificed as part of a clever plan. He moved the rook, but Eliza ignored the bait. She moved her queen instead.

'Moving your rook was a big mistake,' she said. 'You should have taken notice of Bottles. Now you have a problem you are not going to get out of.'

Eliza was right, and the game soon ended, and she was the winner again.

'You are a brutal chess player,' said Jake.

Eliza laughed. 'I warned you. I don't like to lose. Kids won't play me anymore. Dad is the only one who will play me, and he is teaching me new things all the time.'

Jake found himself reflecting back to the day they first met, when he thought she was just a dumb kid who did not know how to catch fish. He now knew better. She was a competitive daredevil who hated to lose, had a forgiving nature, and was full of surprises, including a high tolerance for the smell of rotting seaweed.

Bottles pointed to the chess set and then to himself. 'Would you like a game, Bottles?' Eliza asked.

Bottles nodded, so Eliza set up the pieces once more. Who would you like to play?' she said.

Bottles pointed to her and so began the game. Jake watched what was to become a drawn-out battle of wits with Bottles the victor. 'Wow,' said Eliza. 'You are good. I bet my dad would like to play you sometime.'

Bottles nodded, and the kids could tell by his eyes, that he was smiling.

The afternoon was getting late, so the kids left Bottles to enjoy the aroma of rotting seaweed on his own. They headed for Eliza's corner where Jake left her with the wireless and basket. Then he pedalled home with the chess set under his arm, but along the way he had a brainwave. His dad would never approve of Eliza as a normal friend, but what if she came under the guise of being his chess coach?

27

THE MYSTERY DOOR

When Jake set out for Eliza's house the next day, he first rode past the Old Jetty just in case she was already there, and she was. The day was hot and so was her bedroom, so she had come to the beach early. Jake rang his bicycle bell three times, and she waved. The bicycle bell was the new code, chosen by Eliza because she thought Jake's motorbike sound was silly.

Jake hid his bike and made his way along the seawall, thinking Eliza would be under the jetty by the time he got there, but she stayed put until he arrived. Only once he was there, did she make a move. She scrambled over their seaweed wall to where Jake was waiting. 'I was scared to be under here on my own,' she said, keeping her voice low.

'What is there to be scared of?' asked Jake.

'Shush,' she whispered, and then she pointed to the mystery door. It was slightly ajar. 'I think someone might be in there listening to us.'

The kids looked at the door, its purpose known only to the Army. Their first instinct was to leave, but they hesitated. They had stumbled upon an opportunity to solve a mystery that had baffled everyone they knew.

'I am going to see what the Army hide behind that door,' said Eliza.

Jake was equally as curious, but Eliza was clearly the dare devil of the two. 'But what if someone is in there?' he asked.

'I will knock first.'

'But what if a baddie comes out and grabs you?'

'Then you will have to save me.'

Jake thought about that part of Eliza's plan. Saving her from the clutches of an evil villain might be a task beyond him. They needed a better idea. 'I will be the one to go,' he said, 'and you can be the lookout. If something bad happens, scream your lungs out and run for help.'

Eliza nodded and stood ready to run, as she watched Jake creep towards the door. He peered through the opening but saw only darkness. 'Is anybody home?' he asked, and then he gave a soft knock.

No answer.

He knocked louder and said in a much bolder voice, 'Hello.'

Still no answer.

Jake gave the door a gentle push, and to his surprise, it swung all the way open. *A door that is never used should be stiff on its hinges*, he thought. He looked in, expecting that it might be an entrance to a tunnel, but what he saw was a room. He reached inside the door and found a light switch. It worked. A light came on and Jake guessed that he was looking into some type of an air raid shelter or bunker. The first things he noticed were two glazed picture frames hanging on one of the walls. The frames displayed the black silhouetted images of World War II planes, and he guessed that knowing their shapes would have been vital knowledge for gunners at the time. Deciding which planes to leave and which to shoot down would have been an important feature of their job. But stuck to another wall was something out of place. It was a circus poster, the same as the ones Eliza and he had been putting up a few days before.

The bunker seemed deserted. 'I'm going inside for a better look,' said Jake, no longer bothering to whisper. 'Warn me if someone is coming.'

'Be careful,' said Eliza.

'I will.'

Jake stepped in and looked about. The place seemed well ventilated, not damp and musky as its location suggested. But the lack of a window gave the room a gloomy aura. In one corner was a bed, and next to it was a wooden chest. In the opposite corner stood a small cupboard on which was a Bakelite telephone and a kerosene stove.

Jake felt as if he had stepped into a time capsule. He stood there, thinking about those who would have served in that place during the war, but then he wondered about the circus poster. It had been put there recently, which meant that the bunker was still operational.

He inspected the chest and found it to be unlocked, so he peeked inside. There he found two folded blankets, a notebook, and something wrapped in a towel. He opened the notebook, thinking that it might give a clue as to the room's purpose, but everything was written in verse. Jake guessed that the poems were some sort of a secret code that the army used to disguise important information. However, as he turned the pages, something fell out. It was a photo of a much younger Miss Brown. It appeared that his Sunday School teacher had been one of those involved with the bunker those many years ago.

Then Jake unwrapped the towel, and what he discovered sent a shiver down his spine. It was a service revolver. He laid the ominous object on the bed, his senses telling him that it was time to leave, but there was one more thing he wanted to check. If the room was operational, then the telephone would still be working. He put the phone to his ear and heard a dial tone, but then his ear detected something moist. He inspected the phone's earpiece and discovered that it was covered in blood. Then he noticed a trail of blood on the floor. 'Run!' he yelled to Eliza as he rushed out of the room.

Jake did not bother to sneak along the sea wall this time. He followed Eliza up the jetty stairs instead, and to his horror, the trail of blood was also on the stairs. 'Why are we running?' asked Eliza, but before Jake could answer, Biggles came roaring up on his motorbike. 'Stop, you two,' he shouted.

They stopped at the top of the stairs, each gasping for breath.

'What are you two running from?' Biggles asked.

'Nothing,' Jake panted.

'Are you coming away from your secret meeting place?'

'What secret meeting place?' Jake asked, trying not to show that the question shocked him. *How come he knows we meet here in secret,* he thought. *I know I am on his watch list, but I didn't think he was watching me that closely.*

'Did you go inside the room?' was Biggles' next question.

Jake was struggling to answer, so Eliza took over. 'So what if we did?' she said. 'The door was open, and we knocked first.'

'That room is top secret,' said Biggles. 'It comes under the control of the Army, and you must never reveal its existence, or tell anyone what is in it. There could be serious consequences if you do.'

'I saw fresh blood in there,' said Jake.

'Are you not listening?' Biggles growled. 'None of this is of your concern. If there is blood in there, it will be dealt with by the proper authorities. You are to say nothing.'

The kids left and headed for the warning seat, leaving Biggles to sort out the Army's problem.

28

THE WIRELESS WIZARD

Jake had always wondered about the mystery door, and now he knew what lay behind it, or did he? He had discovered what appeared to be a World War II bunker, untouched since the day the guns fell silent, yet still serving some secret purpose for the Army. However, its existence was a secret that Eliza and he could never tell, a secret they would have to keep forever. Jake was already under the close watch of Biggles, and now the Army would be watching him too, because he knew their secret.

They arrived at the warning seat where Eliza noticed blood on Jake's ear. 'Is your ear bleeding?' she asked.

'No.'

'Then why is there blood on it?'

Jake put his hand to his ear and discovered the blood. 'It's not my blood,' he said. 'It must have come off a telephone I found in the room. I think something bad just happened in there and I have the victim's blood on me.' He wiped the blood away with his handkerchief.

'Biggles would have seen that blood,' said Eliza, 'but he said nothing. That seems odd to me, because he would have heard how you also had blood on you a few days ago.'

'I don't understand any of it,' said Jake, 'but I think someone just got stabbed in the bunker, and thanks to Hoppy, Biggles is going to blame me.'

'Why, what did you find in the bunker?' asked Eliza.

Jake described the bed, the stove, the revolver, and the code book with Miss Brown's picture in it.

'I don't understand how your Sunday School teacher could be involved with people with guns,' said Eliza.

'I don't know either,' said Jake, 'but I am more worried about Biggles seeing the blood on me because Hoppy says I go around stabbing people.'

'If Biggles thought you had done something bad, he would have arrested you,' Eliza reasoned.

'But what if the crime is outside his jurisdiction,' said Jake. 'It is probably a matter that the Military Police will be dealing with.'

'I don't think the Military Police arrest kids who wander through doors the Army leaves open,' laughed Eliza, 'but there is one thing in there you forgot to tell me. From where I was standing, I could see a circus poster on the wall. Everything else could have been in that room for years, but not that.'

'The Army still uses the room because the telephone works,' said Jake. 'Someone from the Army must have put up the circus poster.'

'Perhaps the bunker is the secret base for an Army spy ring,' suggested Eliza. 'They could be spying on the circus.'

'What about Miss Brown's picture? They might be spying on her too,' said Jake.

'Probably not,' said Eliza. 'I think it is more likely that she is one of their spies.'

Jake paused, as he imagined his Sunday School teacher to be a spy. *Wow,* he thought.

The kids agreed that it was all very weird, and they had no idea who they could trust or even tell what they had found. 'I think we should make the town lookout our new meeting place,' said Eliza, 'because under the jetty has become too dangerous. But the lookout has two lots of stairs, and if we see people coming up one lot, we can escape down the other.'

Jake agreed. 'We should meet there tomorrow, and you can bring the wireless if your dad can fix it.'

'Oh, the wireless is already fixed,' said Eliza, 'and I told Dad where you live. He is going to take it back to your place himself.'

'But he might tell my dad that you and I are friends.'

'No, he won't. I told Dad that your dad doesn't approve of us being friends, and he will keep our secret.'

'What did your dad say when you told him?'

'He just laughed.'

Meanwhile, another mystery was unfolding at Jake's home. It was a Saturday afternoon, and Jake's dad was feeling annoyed. He no longer had a wireless to listen to, which was what he did on a Saturday afternoon. The day felt strange, and it became even stranger when he heard a knock at the front door. He went to the door and there stood a man he had seen many times, but he could not remember where. It was only upon seeing the garbage truck parked in the street, that he realised he was talking to the garbage truck driver.

'I believe this is yours,' said the unexpected visitor, who spoke in a thick, European accent. He handed over the wireless.

'I put that with this week's rubbish,' growled Jake's dad. 'Why are you bringing it back?'

'Because it works now. Take it inside and try it.'

'Who fixed it?'

'A nice wizard.'

'What wizard?'

'The Wireless Wizard. He fixes wirelesses he finds in the dump.'

Jake's dad was thinking that the whole thing was a hoax, but his visitor was answering no more questions. 'Best ask your son about the rubbish dump's Wireless Wizard,' laughed the visitor as he walked back to his truck.

Jake arrived home sometime later and found his dad listening to the wireless. 'This old thing has never worked better,' said his dad. 'The sound is so clear and there is no static at all.'

'Great,' said Jake.

'But I don't understand it,' his dad went on. 'The garbage truck takes it away one day and brings it back the next, and now it works.'

'Perhaps the council has upgraded their garbage collection service,' laughed Jake.

'Don't be silly,' said his dad, 'and I need to ask you a question. Who is the rubbish dump's Wireless Wizard?'

'I have no idea,' Jake replied, all the while doing his best to fight off an urge to smile.

'But the garbage truck driver said you did.'

'Just because he sometimes sees me at the dump doesn't mean I know everyone who goes there.'

'You should make some enquiries.'

'Okay. I will keep my eyes open.'

Jake already knew the answer to the mystery that puzzled his dad, but he could think of nothing to explain the mystery he had uncovered under the Old Jetty.

29

THE MISS BROWN MYSTERY

The following day was Sunday, and for once, Jake was eager to get to Sunday School. Its teacher was now the central figure of a mystery he wanted to solve. Did she know about the bunker, and why was her photo in a chest along with a gun? But he would have to be careful how he went about his enquiries, for Miss Brown was not the person she appeared to be. She was either an Army spy, or someone the Army was spying upon. Either way, what he had uncovered was something Biggles did not wish to handle, probably because the people involved had guns. Jake knew of no one who owned a revolver. Even Biggles never carried one.

For the first time ever, Jake was early for Sunday School, but he soon found that none of the girls were speaking to him. Susie had told how he had pushed her over at the dance class, and his reputation had gone from stinky fish boy to girl basher. With no girls willing to talk, Jake tried the boys, but the result was the same. They would not speak to him either, for none wanted to fall out of favour with Susie because she was part of the Cassidy family and enjoyed the same protection as Hoppy.

Once Sunday School was over for the day, the kids left, but Jake stayed back. 'You are still here, Jake,' said a surprised Miss Brown, who knew that Jake was always the first out the door.

'Er, yes, Miss Brown.'

'I thought you would be gone by now.'

'I have a question.'

'This is very encouraging, Jake. What would you like to know about today's lesson?'

'It's not about that.'

'Oh.'

'It's about an old photo I found. It's a photo of you.'

'I doubt it would be me,' laughed Miss Brown. 'I hate having my photo taken. To find a photo of me would be a rare find indeed.'

'It was a photo taken many years ago, but I can tell it is you.'

'What was I wearing?'

'A dress with butterflies on it.'

'Where was it taken?'

'You were standing on the Old Jetty, very close to where I found it.'

Miss Brown went quiet, and then a strange look came over her face. 'Jake, if you have a photo of me, I would like it back please.'

'I can't give it back.'

'Why?'

'Because I put it back where I found it.'

'And where exactly was that?'

Jake hesitated, not wanting to tell her about the bunker, but then he thought that if she was one of the spies, she would know about it already. 'I found it in your secret room,' he said.

'Jake, I do not have a secret room, and I don't know who told you about that photo, but it was lost years ago. Please don't talk about it again.'

Jake said no more, for Miss Brown had begun to cry. He left quietly, having just become the ultimate outsider. Even his Sunday School teacher no longer wanted to talk to him.

When Jake met Eliza at the lookout that afternoon, she was keen to hear his report, but first he told her how none of the Sunday School kids were speaking to him.

'I can see why you hate going there,' she laughed.

'It's not funny,' said Jake. 'Even Miss Brown doesn't want to speak to me.'

'Wow,' said Eliza. 'You are becoming a real expert at upsetting people.'

'I did nothing to the kids, and all I did to Miss Brown was to ask her about the photo.'

'And what did she say?'

'She said the photo was lost years ago, and then she began to cry.'

'Why would she have cried?' asked Eliza.

'I don't know,' said Jake.

Eliza thought for a moment and came up with a new theory. 'I think the man in the bunker could be a secret agent who has been assigned to get Miss Brown,' she said. 'That is why he has her photo and a gun.'

'Should we go to the police?' said Jake.

'Biggles is the police, and he said we had to stay out of it,' said Eliza.

'But at least we should warn Miss Brown.'

'The bunker belongs to the Army,' Eliza reasoned. 'That means the man in the bunker is on our side. Miss Brown is probably a Russian Spy, and your Sunday School is probably the headquarters of their spy ring.'

'But who can we tell?' said Jake. 'If I tell my parents, Dad will find out about you.'

'Perhaps we could tell Ben,' suggested Eliza.

'I am not sure that we should tell anyone,' Jake replied. 'What say we meet in Ben's shop tomorrow while I think about it some more.'

'Okay,' Eliza replied. 'But we can't just do nothing.'

30

MORE FOUL PLAY

When Jake arrived at the jetty the next morning, he found Hoppy to be in an exceptionally good mood. 'Hey, Jughead,' said Hoppy. 'I guess you won't be handing out anymore Ferris wheel tickets.'

'Why?'

'The authorities have shut down the wheel of death due to safety issues,' Hoppy laughed. 'Dad told me last night. He said that someone had reported something about a bolt being loose.'

'I don't believe you,' said Jake.

Hoppy smirked. 'Go and ask your friend Ben,' he said.

No more was said, but Jake found the smug look on Hoppy's face to be a major source of annoyance for the rest of the morning.

Later that day, Jake and Eliza met as planned in Ben's shop, where Ben confirmed that Hoppy's information was correct. He said that safety experts had gone over the Ferris wheel that morning, looking for defects. Apparently, an anonymous member of the public had reported that a vital bolt, used to hold a seat in place, had come loose.

'Which seat was it?' asked Eliza.

'The yellow one.'

'Eliza and I sat in that seat last week,' said Jake. 'We checked all its bolts and none of them were loose.'

'Do you always check for loose bolts when you hop on a carnival ride?' asked Ben.

'Doesn't everyone?' said Jake.

'Not usually,' Ben chuckled, 'but you can never be too careful.'

Then Ben became more serious. 'The Ferris wheel owner thinks that someone is sending him a sinister message to stop him giving me free Ferris wheel tickets,' he said. 'Apparently, the safety inspectors could tell that the bolt had been loosened with a spanner.'

'Your friend could be right,' said Jake. 'And if the person with the spanner knows that Eliza and I like to ride in the yellow seat, the message could be for us as well.'

'Could be,' said Ben. 'Councillor Cassidy has spies everywhere, but what he has done was stupid. The Ferris wheel is already back in business, while he has made an enemy of its owner. From now on, the Ferris wheel will have a night watchman, and I will still be getting all the tickets I want.'

'Talking about spies,' said Eliza.

'No, let's not,' said Jake. 'Warn Ben about the Wireless Wizard instead.'

'Who is the Wireless Wizard?' asked Ben.

'If Dad comes in and asked anything about the rubbish dump's Wireless Wizard, tell him you don't know who he is,' said Jake.

'That will be easy,' Ben replied, 'because I have never heard of him.'

'The Wireless Wizard is my dad,' said Eliza, brimming with pride. 'I gave him Jake's wireless and he fixed it, but keep it a secret because Jake is banned from seeing me.'

'Got it,' said Ben, 'but can your dad fix any wireless?'

'Sure can.'

Ben seemed interested. 'Perhaps your dad could drop into the shop sometime,' he said. 'I might be able to help him with a small business opportunity.'

'Then Ben had more good news, and added, 'You don't have to worry about Councillor Casidy's secret witness who saw you near Hoppy's bike. The secret witness is Bottles. The councillor claims that when he asked Bottles if he had seen anyone near Hoppy's bike that morning, Bottles had said, "Jug", which is what kids call you.'

'Bottles would have been saying *Ug*, not Jug,' said Jake, 'because that is how he answers every question.'

'I know,' laughed Ben, 'and so does Officer Biggs. The whole thing was just a bluff by the councillor. He wanted Officer Biggs to accuse your mum of lying about the alibi she gave you.'

'I thought Biggles was too honest to go along with something like that,' said Jake.

'I wouldn't blame Officer Biggs,' said Ben, 'because Councillor Cassidy has some sort of a hold over him. The officer must do whatever the councillor tells him, but the councillor didn't tell him that the secret witness was Bottles. The officer only found that out today, and he said that he was going around to apologise to your mum because someone had told him how upset he had made her.'

'It was me who complained to Biggles for upsetting Mum,' said Jake.

'Good for you,' laughed Ben.

'Can we tell you a secret?' asked Eliza. 'It's a secret that Biggles said we can tell no one.'

Jake frowned at her.

Eliza frowned back.

'What is the secret?' Ben asked.

'Jake doesn't want me to say but I think we should, because I don't trust Biggles.'

Ben looked at Jake. 'What do you think?' he asked.

'We will tell you what we know, but we can't tell you how we found out,' said Jake. 'It's about Miss Brown. We think she is a spy.'

Ben raised his eyebrows and peered over the rim of his glasses. 'A spy, you say?'

'We think she is under the surveillance of the Army,' said Eliza.

'Perhaps she is spying for the Russians,' chuckled Ben.

'Probably,' Eliza replied. 'Someone from the Army has her photo and is looking for her with a gun, but you can tell none of this to anyone.'

'Believe me, I won't tell a soul,' laughed Ben, 'but do you mind if I just happen to mention it to my wife tonight. She thinks nothing funny ever happens in this shop, and I am always trying to convince her otherwise.'

The kids looked at each other, their faces blank. It appeared that they would have to keep the secret to themselves, for no one was ever going to believe them anyway.

31

JAKE TO THE RESCUE

Jake's family were having their evening meal when Ben called in with more interesting news. 'Officer Biggs now has a new suspect in the Hoppy attempted murder case,' he said. 'It appears that a kid wearing a t-shirt with a number six on it, had been seen tampering with Hoppy's bike that morning. Do you know anyone who wears a shirt like that?' he asked Jake.

'That sounds like Eliza's brother,' Jake replied.

'Then someone needs to warn him,' said Ben. 'Officer Biggs will be checking the jetties in the morning, looking for any kid wearing a t-shirt like that. Eliza's brother needs to ditch it.'

'I will get the word to him,' said Jake.

'Stop right there,' said Jake's dad. 'I don't approve of you interfering in a criminal investigation, and I want to know who Eliza is? You know I don't approve of you associating with girls, because girls will interfere with your education.'

'But Eliza is my chess coach,' said Jake. 'She is helping me with my education. Her father was the national chess champion in her home country.'

But Jake's dad was not buying it. 'Where do you go for these chess lessons?' he asked.

'I see Eliza in Ben's shop.'

Ben nodded. 'Eliza and Jake meet in my shop from time to time, and she seems a very bright girl.'

Jake's dad shook his head, but his mum had something to say. 'I think Jake having chess lessons is a good idea,' she said. 'His report card says that he needs to improve his chess playing skills, and I think we are lucky that this girl is prepared to help him.'

Silence followed, as everyone waited for Jake's dad to pronounce his judgement. Then came the decision. 'Alright, Jake can see this girl in Ben's shop for chess lessons, but nowhere else, and he must promise not to warn her brother. If he does, I will withdraw my permission.'

Jake agreed to his dad's terms, knowing that seeing Eliza was going to be very tricky from now on. That night, he lay in bed, wondering what to do, but there appeared to be only one option. He would have to go to the Old Jetty the next morning, despite the hostility he would find there. However, if things went right, he would run into Eliza as if by accident, and could tell her to warn Ivan. That way, none of his dad's rules would be broken.

Jake was first to arrive at the Old Jetty the next morning, where he waited for the sunrise. In the past, that jetty had been a happy place for him, but it was now enemy territory. He felt uneasy, just standing there, all alone, looking towards the darkened houses of the Workers Village. The enemy were about to leave those houses, and they would be coming to where he was standing. He would be surrounded. His plan was to save Ivan, but first he would have to talk to Eliza. With him was Timmy, who was on his last chance to prove himself a guard dog.

Then Timmy scored a mark in his favour, being first to detect the approach of the enemy. 'Woof!' he barked as the group of shadowy figures came towards them, their darkened silhouettes standing out against the glow of the red sunrise. Then Jake saw them too. Kids on bikes, and as they got closer, he could see a yellow hat.

Timmy charged the group as they got off their bikes, and he singled out Eliza. He jumped up on her, expecting a pat, and she was surprised to see him. She scuffed his ears and whispered, 'Where is Jake?'

'Woof,' was Timmy's reply, and then he ran back to his master.

Ivan saw Timmy and then saw Jake. 'Hey, fellas, the moron from the Town Jetty is back with his stupid dog,' he shouted.

Jake's chance of talking to Eliza was gone.

'What are you here for?' growled Ivan.

Fortunately, Jake had anticipated that Ivan would be wearing his blue t-shirt, and he had come with another for Ivan to put on. However, Ivan was never going to do that without a good reason, and Jake was forbidden to tell him that Biggles was on the hunt that morning.

'I want to make a trade with you, but you have to do it now,' said Jake.

'What sort of a trade?'

Jake pulled a t-shirt from out of his tackle box. 'I will swap you this brand-new t-shirt for the old one you are wearing.'

'Why?'

'I can't say.'

'Why not?'

'I can't tell you why, because I have promised someone that I wouldn't, but I need a shirt with number six on the back. Just trust me, and if you are not happy, we can swap back tomorrow.'

'No, so I give you to the count of five to get off this jetty.'

Jake reached into his pocket and pulled out his opera glasses. 'What if I give you these opera glasses as well?' he said.

'Are you stupid?' said Ivan. 'Those things look expensive.'

Jake could hear Biggles' motorbike coming along the esplanade. 'My offer goes to the count of three,' he said. 'Take it now or you will be the one who looks stupid. One. Two. Thre—'

'Okay, gimme your stuff, but I don't get it.'

The swap was made, and only just in time, for Biggles' motorbike came rattling over the jetty planks.

'I am looking for a boy wearing a blue t-shirt with the number six on the back,' said Biggles. 'Has anyone seen a shirt like that?'

Everyone remained silent, but then Timmy growled. He had something in his mouth that he had just found in Jake's tackle box. It was the number six t-shirt.

Biggles grabbed hold of it, but Timmy was not letting go.

'Give it here!'

'Grr.'

A tug-of-war followed, then Timmy gave in, surrendering the damning piece of evidence to Biggles.

'There are no kids with a number six t-shirt here,' said Eliza.'
'Would a dog do?'

'Don't be smart with me, lassie,' said Biggles. 'I saw where the t-shirt came from. Who owns that tackle box.'

'It's mine,' said Jake, 'but I don't know much about the t-shirt. It's just a rag I'm using to wipe my hands on while I am fishing.'

Biggles sniffed the shirt, and sure enough, it smelt like everyone had been wiping their hands on it, which is what happens when someone wears the same shirt fishing every day.

'We all use that rag,' said Eliza. 'It's common property.'

'I told you not to be smart with me,' came the blunt reply.

'You said you were looking for a boy,' said Jake. 'Why are you picking on a girl?'

'Listen carefully, Jake Jones,' said Biggles. 'Everyone knows that it was you who loosened the generator on Gerald's bike, and you were wearing this t-shirt at the time. Confess now, and the law will go easy on you, because some are calling your crime an act of attempted murder.'

It was then that Ivan realised that Jake was trying to save him from the law, despite being the one the law blamed for Ivan's crime. He needed to help. 'Give us back our wiping rag,' he said. 'I found it on the beach, and we all use it.'

'That's right,' said another kid. 'It's ours, so give it back.'

The kids began to chant, 'Give us back our wiping rag.'

Biggles had always done his best to gain the trust of the immigrant kids, and he did not want to lose it over a silly t-shirt. 'Sorry, kids,' he said. 'I am looking for the person who once wore this shirt, but I am sure that it was none of you.' Then Eliza began to giggle. 'What are you laughing at, young lady?' Biggles asked.

Eliza stopped giggling. 'We have to say that we are sorry too,' she said. 'Our doggie just did a wee on your tyre.'

Biggles glared at the offending animal, but Timmy just stood there looking innocent. Had Timmy been a person, he could have been arrested, but his four-legged status gave him immunity. However, as Biggles went to leave, he said, 'Don't bother coming back here tomorrow, because the jetty will be closed. You will have to do your fishing from the Town Jetty.'

The kids watched the motorbike as it rattled once more over the jetty planks, but Biggles' departing words made no sense. It was Timmy who had done a wee on his tyre, yet he was punishing them all by telling them that they had to fish from the Town Jetty. It was as if he wanted the jetty war to erupt full scale.

Ivan shook Jake by the hand. 'Thanks,' he said. 'We won't give you any more trouble from now on, but the jetty war is not yet over. If Biggles makes us go to the Town Jetty, it is going to be World War III.' Then he gave Jake back his opera glasses. 'You can have your shirt back tomorrow,' he said. 'I need it today, so I don't get sunburnt.'

'Thanks,' said Jake, who had good reason to be pleased. He had saved Ivan from the law, and he had done it without breaking the promise he made to his dad. Added to this, Eliza and he could now fish from the same jetty, and his dad could not object if they both just happened to be there at the same time.

32

THE CRAB NET

Eliza was happy, for Ivan and Jake were now friends, and Jake could stay on a day when she needed his help. Her dad had given her his crab net and asked her to catch him some crabs, but she had no idea what to do. She had asked Ivan for help, but he said it would interfere with his fishing. 'Can you help me please?' she asked Jake.

Had anyone else asked Jake to forsake fishing that morning, he would have been like Ivan and refused. However, for Eliza, he was prepared to make the sacrifice. 'Sure, I've caught hundreds of crabs,' he said.

'You are an expert then?'

'I am, but we need to go further up the jetty.'

'Okay.'

Jake chose a spot where the water was deeper. 'Did your dad give you any crab bait?' he asked.

Eliza produced a bone from her tackle box and put it next to the crab net, where it remained for barely a second. 'Timmy! come back with my bone,' she shouted, but Timmy would hear none of it. He bolted for home. 'Stop that dog,' yelled Eliza to the kids who were fishing closer to shore.

The kids formed a human wall, causing the fugitive dog to apply the brakes and double back. Jake caught him, but Timmy was not giving up. That bone was a gourmet treat to a dog, but to a Human, it was just a bone. To deprive him of something for which Jake had no true appreciation, was not fair. Timmy hung on to his prize.

'Let go, Timmy,' growled Jake.

'Grr,' growled the deprived dog.

'Let go!'

Finally, Timmy surrendered the bone, then wagged his tail as if all was forgiven. However, he soon became concerned when he saw Jake tie the bone into the crab net, then even more concerned when Jake threw the crab net into the water. A juicy bone being dispatched in such a bizarre fashion, was hard for a dog to witness. The bone disappeared, lost at sea, somewhere at the bottom of the ocean.

Jake and Eliza joined the other kids, leaving Timmy to stare over the side, looking for a bone that was somewhere in the depths below. Then a few minutes later, they returned, and Jake began to pull up the net, much to Timmy's excitement. He sprang to attention for his bone was being rescued. Moments later, the crab net was on the jetty, but a strange creature was now guarding the bone. Timmy growled at it, for it was small enough for a dog to handle, but it was feisty and came armed with deadly weapons. The crab menaced them, lashing out with open nippers, so Timmy decided to let Jake deal with whatever it was.

Jake grabbed the crab by its flippers, rendering it harmless, but the crab was not giving in. It seized the bone, intent on inflicting an injury, but its choice of victim made no sense at all. Finally, the bone was released, and Jake threw the grumpy crab over the side. 'Too small,' he said. 'It's against the law to catch them that size.'

Eliza watched her crab swim away. 'Are you sure it was too small?' she asked.

'Don't worry,' said Jake. 'We will try further along the jetty where the crabs might be bigger.'

Jake chose another spot, but Timmy did not want to see his bone thrown back into the water again. In an act of desperation, he tried to grab it out of the net, but Jake saw him lunge and quickly heaved the net over the side. Everything finished up in the water, including the end of the rope that should have been tied to the jetty rail.

'How are we supposed to pull the crab net in?' asked Eliza.

'Bad dog. Look what you made me do,' growled Jake, but Eliza saw Jake as the culprit.

'You just threw Dad's crab net away,' she said.

Jake watched everything sink to the bottom. Eliza was right. The crab net was lost, and Eliza was upset. She began to sob. 'Dad is going to be mad at me when he finds out that I have lost his crab net,' she mumbled.

Jake's heart sank, for he had made Eliza cry. He needed to make amends, but deep water was the shark's territory. *Only a fool would dive in after that net,* he thought.

'I wish Gorilla Boy was here,' sobbed Eliza. 'He would get that net for me.'

She was well aware of the resentment Jake felt towards the infamous circus star, and her comment touched a nerve. Jake's manhood was being questioned.

'Wait here while I go home and get my snorkelling gear,' he said, as he was thinking, *That stupid Gorilla Boy probably can't even swim.*

'Okay. I will make sure no one else dives in and gets the net while you are gone,' said Eliza.

As if, thought Jake. He hopped on his bike and headed for home.

33

A DIVE INTO SHARK TERRITORY

It was not long before Jake was back, dressed only in bathers and carrying his snorkelling gear. Not surprisingly, Timmy was no longer with him, for his performance that morning had been deemed unsatisfactory, other than for when he had tinkled on Biggles' tyre.

Jake put on his snorkelling gear. 'Keep a lookout for sharks,' he said.

'What do I do if I see one?'

'Yell out to me.'

'But what if you don't hear me?'

'Yell louder.'

Jake's plan should a shark appear, was not a good one, and his next plan was no better. To reach the water he had to climb down the ladder, and the last time he did that, he had messed up his Sunday School clothes. Fortunately, he was wearing bathers this time, so nothing bad was likely to happen.

He climbed over the jetty rail and placed a foot on the top rung of the ladder, but that was as far as he got. From there, he hit the water with a mighty splash, resolving never again to wear flippers while descending a ladder. Fortunately, he managed to hang on to his snorkel and mask, and the offending flippers were still on his feet. The ladder had proved to be his nemesis again.

It took all Eliza's willpower not to laugh. 'Are you okay?' she shouted.

'Yes,' came the spluttered reply.

'Good,' she said, and then she could hold back her laughter no more, much to Jake's annoyance.

Jake had never snorkelled at the end of a jetty before because he considered deep water to be the territory of sharks, but he soon discovered why it appealed to so many divers. What he saw was far more spectacular than expected. The seabed beneath the jetty was not all sand, but was partly reef, and from it rose a colourful array of seaweed. The piles that supported the jetty were equally as spectacular, for they were encrusted with marine growth, and every pile hosted a school of tiny fish. The fish stayed close to the piles, seeking protection from predators, so Jake decided to do the same. He swam beneath the jetty, thinking that having piles on either side was safer than swimming in open water.

He headed for the place where the net had been lost, but so fascinated was he by all that he saw, that he almost forgot what he was there for. He watched the seaweed that rose from the reef outcrops, gently swaying back and forth to the rhythm of the waves. Then a crab sprung from nowhere, displaying its nippers in an act of defiance. Further along, several bits of seaweed caught his eye. They seemed to be detached from the bottom, but strangely, they were not being carried away by the current. He dived down to have a closer look, and what he found were creatures unknown to him. They had the heads of seahorses, but they swam with fins that made them look more like bits of seaweed.

Eliza shouted from above. 'The net is just out from where you are.'

Jake would have liked to have stayed longer with the strange creatures, but the chance of meeting a shark increased with every minute that he was in the water. He swam out and found the net, but that was the easy part. News of the bone had spread throughout the crab world, and the net was now full of them.

'Have you got the net?' called Eliza.

'No.'

'Why not?'

'It's full of crabs.'

'How many?'

'Five I think.'

'Fantastic. Dad will be pleased.'

Jake did not answer, because he was not prepared to retrieve a net full of crabs. He had seen how their nippers could latch on to a bone, and any mistake on his part would be painful.

He dived down and kicked his flippers, hoping that a swirl of water would frighten the crabs away, but it was a mistake. On his next dive, he could see nothing at all. His flippers had stirred up a cloud of sand, and somewhere in that cloud lurked five angry crabs. He swam back to the surface, now less worried about sharks, but suddenly fearful that five sets of powerful nippers were after him.

'Have you got the net yet?' called Eliza.

'No.'

'Why not?'

'It's too dangerous.'

'I bet Gorilla Boy could get it.'

That bragging, lying, gorilla fraud would probably cry if he got his feet wet, thought Jake, but this was not the time to discuss the virtues of Gorilla Boy. 'I will try something different,' he shouted.

Jake found the end of the rope and tied it around his waist, then began to swim back to the ladder, but towing the net in this fashion made the going slow. His fear of sharks returned, and he thought that perhaps it was karma. Like the gents he used for bait, he was now the one attached to the end of a line, struggling in an ocean full of things that could eat him. 'Are you still looking out for sharks?' he called to Eliza.

'Yes,' she said, 'but you could swim a lot faster if you held the net in your hand.'

Jake did not bother to explain the problem.

After what proved to be an exhausting swim, he reached the ladder, this time taking off his flippers before making the climb.

'You let the crabs get away,' said Eliza.

'Don't worry, we will just have to catch some more,' said Jake.

Then Eliza said, 'You don't like Gorilla Boy very much, do you, Jake?'

'No, why, do you?'

'Not really. Sorry I mentioned him. He probably can't even swim.'

Jake smiled to himself, and the rest of the morning was all good. By lunch time, they had more than enough crabs to make Eliza's dad happy.

34

THE WIRE FENCE

Jake was now welcome on both jetties, a privilege that no other kid enjoyed, but he would have to be careful. If Hoppy were to discover that he fished with the enemy, he would call Jake a traitor in a further attempt to destroy his reputation. However, Jake thought it was a risk worth taking, for fishing with Eliza meant more to him than worrying about the opinion of friends who were fickle. But when he arrived at the Old Jetty the next day, things were not the same. A wire fence had been erected part way along, preventing people from going further. The fence had a locked gate, and on it was a sign.

JETTY CLOSED

NO ACCESS BEYOND THIS POINT

A fine of £10 applies

The Old Jetty Gang were gathered at the fence, recalling how Biggles had told them that they would find the jetty closed when next they came, but still they were shocked to see that it had actually happened. However, it was only a wire fence with no barbed wire at the top. Such a fence could never stop a kid, and Ivan was the first to climb over it. The rest followed.

They began fishing, but soon heard a familiar noise. Biggles was on his motorbike, doing his morning patrol along the esplanade. 'Did anybody read the bit about a ten-pound fine?' said one of the kids.

'I think that only applies to grownups,' said another.

'Who cares?' said Ivan. 'No one I know has ten pounds. They might as well make it a thousand. They are never going to get any money.'

'But if you can't pay, they send you to jail,' said a kid.

'Only if they catch you,' laughed Ivan.

'But Biggles can see us out here and we have nowhere to escape.'

The kid was right. They were sitting ducks. Everyone began to think about the possible outcome. Would they be going to court? Could they be asked to pay a fine by instalments? Would their parents be made to pay? Would the jetty ever be open again?

The motorbike reached the jetty and stopped, and the kids could see Biggles looking directly at them. Then he looked around, as if checking to see who else was about. As always, the streets were deserted at that time of morning, but what Biggles did next, came as a surprise. He gave the kids a friendly wave and rode on, causing everyone to breathe a collective sigh of relief. Perhaps he was not such a bad cop after all.

That afternoon, Jake and Eliza met in Ben's shop for what would be Jake's first official chess lesson. They told Ben about the fence, but he already knew. His customers had been complaining about it all day, but it was the mayor's visit that had Ben the most worried. It appeared that Councillor Cassidy had organised for the fence to be put there, and that he intended to have the jetty demolished.

The mayor had said that for many years, Councillor Cassidy had wanted the jetty to go, so that the money spent on its annual upkeep could better be used to support a proposed holiday village on land that he owned. However, the holiday village project had never gone ahead because the cost to demolish the jetty could not be justified, a situation that had always angered the councillor. So to appease him, the council had given its permission for him to demolish the jetty if he did the job himself. However, that permission was given before the Workers Village had grown to accommodate the new arrivals. The Old Jetty now served a new purpose, for it was the only public asset the new arrivals had.

The mayor had gone on to tell Ben that the council was planning to withdraw its permission at its next meeting, which was in two days' time. As a result, he thought that Councillor Cassidy had decided to start demolition now, but the mayor was not worried. He said that not much could happen in two days, as demolition would take several weeks.

'What will happen to the seahorses if they take away their home?' asked Eliza.

'What seahorses?' asked Ben.

'There are seahorses living under the Old Jetty,' said Jake, 'but they disguise themselves to look like bits of seaweed.'

Ben pulled out a fish identification book that he kept in the shop. 'Let's see what pictures of seahorses we have in here,' he said.

Jake looked over Ben's shoulder as he turned to the seahorse page. 'Are any of these your seahorses?' he asked.

Jake looked at the seahorses and was surprised by how many different types there were, but only one looked like his. 'That one,' he said, pointing to a picture.

'Are you sure?' asked Ben.

'Definitely,' said Jake.

Ben read the description. 'It says they are called Leafy Seadragons, and they are quite rare. I think we should tell the museum about them.'

Ben rang the museum and spoke to a rather sceptical professor, who said he would look into the matter when he was not so busy. It was only when Ben told him that he thought they might start to demolish the jetty the next day, that the professor said he would come first thing in the morning.

'Do you think the professor could stop them from demolishing the jetty?' asked Jake.

'I don't think professors have a lot of power in that department,' replied Ben. 'We will just have to wait and see.'

35

LEAFY SEADRAGONS

Jake and Eliza were waiting on the footpath when Ben arrived to open his shop the next day, because they did not want to miss the visit of the professor. Each had their own idea of what a professor would look like, Jake imagining him to have unkempt hair, a bit like Albert Einstein, while Eliza thought he would be a well-spoken gentleman dressed in a suit. Neither was correct.

A stout gentleman with a bald head, walked into the shop. He was wearing a striped pair of bathers and a Hawaiian t-shirt. Under his arm he carried a book.

'You must be the professor,' said Ben.

'I am Professor Hubert Smithers, and you would be the person I spoke to yesterday,' said the professor. He spoke in a pompous tone.

'We did speak yesterday, and you can call me Ben,' said Ben.

Jake and Eliza had a quiet giggle, but fortunately, the professor did not notice. It was only the kids in the room who knew that Hubert Smithers was the name of the cynical butler in the Archie comic books.

'You say a couple of kids saw a seahorse under a jetty,' said the professor. 'I consider that most unlikely, but it would be remiss of me not to investigate seeing that you are telling me that the jetty is about to be demolished.'

'Good,' said Ben. 'These two are Jake and Eliza. Jake is the one who saw the seahorse.'

'I saw more than one,' said Jake, excited to be telling a man of science about his discovery.

The professor looked at him with an intimidating frown, which was something Jake had become accustomed to since becoming a student at his grandpa's old college. 'I doubt that you saw a seahorse, lad, but let me show you some pictures.' The professor had the same book that

144

Ben had in his shop, and he turned to the same page and pointed to a seahorse. 'Is that what you saw?' he asked.

'Not really,' said Jake.

'Oh, so you are wasting my time then. I should have known better than to come here. That is the only seahorse known to live in this part of the world.'

The professor definitely reminded Jake of one of his teachers, and it was not a teacher that he liked.

'I saw the seahorse that wears the seaweed disguise,' said Jake.

'Seahorses don't wear disguises,' scoffed the professor.

Jake pointed to the picture of the Leafy Seadragon. 'I saw that one,' he said.

The professor shook his head. 'I doubt that would be the case,' he smirked. 'That is a Leafy Seadragon. I personally have never seen one because they are quite rare and don't live around here.'

'They do,' insisted Jake. 'I have my snorkelling gear with me, and I can show you where they live.'

'All right,' said the professor. 'I have come dressed for a swim and have my diving gear in the car. Not that I expect that you will be showing me much, but it is a nice day to be out of the office.'

The kids jumped into the professor's car, and they drove to the Old Jetty. 'I normally leave this diving stuff to my students,' said the professor, 'but they are all on holidays at this time of year.' He grabbed his snorkelling gear from the boot. 'Lead the way, lad,' he said, and they walked towards the water.

Jake noticed that the professor had a hand spear. 'What is that for?' he asked, thinking that the professor might be planning to spear a Seadragon.

'Sharks,' said the professor. 'I feel more comfortable having a spear with me when I am diving.'

Jake thought that his fear of sharks was something to be ashamed of, but apparently not. *I need to get myself a hand spear*, he thought.

Then, just as Jake and the professor were about to enter the water, a man yelled from the jetty. 'No swimming is allowed near this jetty. This is a demolition site.'

The mayor's suspicion had been confirmed, and demolition was about to start.

'Get lost,' shouted Jake.

'If you swim near the jetty, I am calling the police,' yelled the man.

'We may have to do what he says,' said the professor.

'Don't worry about him,' Jake replied. 'Our local copper never books people.'

The professor hesitated, but Jake waded into the water. 'Come on,' he said. 'This might be the only chance you will ever get to see a Leafy Seadragon.'

Eliza noticed that the gate in the fence was open, so she decided to take a walk along the jetty, but the same man stopped her. 'Can't you read, stupid child. The sign says you can't go past the fence, so go back.' Eliza did not know it then, but the man shouting at everyone that morning was Councillor Cassidy. She went back and sat on the seawall, waiting for Jake and the professor to return.

Jake and the professor swam out to where the Seadragons lived, then both took their first dive to the bottom. Again, Jake was impressed by the variety of seaweed and shellfish, but the professor was seeing much more, for he knew the scientific names for them all. They were what he studied, and some were not what he would have expected to find under that jetty. Meanwhile, Jake was amazed at how much safer it felt when swimming with a buddy, although a buddy only halved his chances of being eaten by a shark, but then he thought about the spear. Only his buddy had one, which meant that only his buddy could defend himself. Jake's chance of being eaten by a shark was probably the same as always.

It was on their second dive that the professor thought he had died and gone to heaven. They rose to the surface. 'Did you see that!' he exclaimed. 'There are Leafy Seadragons down there.'

As if you are telling me something I didn't already know, Jake mused to himself, but he stayed polite. 'I saw them too,' he said.

'I wish I had brought my underwater camera,' said the professor. 'I will be back tomorrow to take pictures.'

'Better be early,' said Jake. 'They may well have started to demolish the place by then.'

36

DRASTIC ACTION

Jake and the professor swam back to the beach and found Councillor Cassidy and Biggles waiting. 'I should have known that you would be involved, Jake Jones,' said Biggles.

'Hi, Officer Biggs,' said Jake. 'I was just showing the professor the seahorses that live under the jetty.'

'They are actually Leafy Seadragons,' said the professor. 'They are very rare and this jetty needs to be declared a Seadragon sanctuary.'

'I don't care what they are,' said Councillor Cassidy. 'You were told that you could not swim near the jetty.'

'But I wish to return tomorrow to photograph what I have found,' said the professor.

The councillor turned to Biggles. 'Tell him what will happen if he does,' he snapped, but Biggles hesitated. 'Go on, tell him,' the councillor repeated.

'I will be forced to fine you, and perhaps even take you into custody if you fail to follow a legal direction,' said Biggles.

'What legal direction?' asked the professor.

'Tell him,' the councillor said once more.

'I am advising you that you cannot swim within fifty yards of the jetty,' said Biggles.

'Until when?' asked the professor.

'Until forever,' laughed Councillor Cassidy, a smug smile appearing on his face. 'That is because the jetty will soon be gone forever.'

A short time later, everyone gathered back in Ben's shop. 'I thought you said your town policeman never books anyone,' said the professor.

'He lets people off with a warning,' Jake replied, 'but you might become the exception.'

'Why is that?'

'Because Biggles does whatever Councillor Cassidy tells him.'

Ben nodded. 'Councillor Cassidy runs this town, and when people don't do as he says, he finds ways to make life difficult for them. I would be careful if I were you because that man has friends in high places.'

'I certainly don't want to do anything that might bring shame to the museum,' said the professor, 'but we need to save those Seadragons. I have friends in the newspaper business, and I think everyone needs to read about the threat that hangs over your rare creatures.'

The professor bid them farewell, but Ben was more worried than ever. 'We have to get the town on side,' he said, because Councillor Cassidy might do something drastic before the council have a chance to stop him.'

The kids decided to take drastic action of their own, for they had to get the word out, and the best way to do that was to talk to every shopkeeper in town. That way, their customers would get to hear about the plight of the Old Jetty. But it would mean Jake and Eliza being seen together in public, and Jake's dad probably hearing about it. The stakes were high, but the kids were on the most important mission of their lives. They started at the newspaper shop because that was where people came for their news.

'What do you children want?' asked a rather grumpy lady who was standing behind the counter of the newspaper shop.

'We want you to tell everyone that the Old Jetty is about to be demolished,' said Eliza.

'Why should I tell them that?'

'Because it is a wonderful jetty that people love.'

'Not anymore,' grumped the shopkeeper. 'The place has been taken over by foreigners and no-hopers. Sensible people don't go there anymore.'

'My family are among those foreigners you are talking about, and we love that jetty,' said Eliza, who could feel herself becoming angry.

'Your family will just have to travel a little further and use the Town Jetty,' was the unsympathetic reply.

'The Town Jetty kids stop the Workers Village kids from going there,' growled Eliza.

'Not my problem,' said the shopkeeper. 'Obviously, you foreign kids have been doing things to upset the locals.'

Eliza stormed out of the shop, and for a second time, Jake saw her cry, but at least it was not him who had caused it this time. Then she regained her composure. 'We have to do this a different way,' she said. 'Sam and Violet went to a ban the bomb rally the other day. A whole lot of teenagers from the university were there, demanding that the atomic bomb be banned.'

'Are they going to ban it?' asked Jake.

'I don't think so,' said Eliza, 'but that is probably because Australia doesn't have a bomb to ban.'

'Then why are they protesting?'

'Because staging a protest is what people do these days, so we need to stage a protest to save the Old Jetty.'

'But we don't go to university,' said Jake. 'Who are we going to get to join our protest?'

'If we hurry, we can ask the Town Jetty kids before they go home,' said Eliza.

'You will have to be the one who asks them?' said Jake.

'Why can't you ask?'

'Because it's your idea and I don't know anything about protests.'

'Okay,' said Eliza, hoping that Jake would change his mind when the time came.

37

AN UNLIKELY ALLY

As they headed for the Town Jetty, Jake had a sudden thought. 'They probably won't believe us?' he said.

'Why wouldn't they?' asked Eliza. 'They are your friends.'

'Boof is my only good friend,' said Jake. 'The rest take notice of Hoppy, and he will say that we are telling lies. He likes turning the other kids against me.'

'We need a Bible then,' said Eliza.

'Why?'

'I have heard that if someone swears on a Bible, it means they are telling the truth.'

'Okay,' said Jake. 'Let's ask Ben if he has one in his shop.'

They raced back to Ben's shop. 'Hi, Ben, got a Bible we can borrow,' Jake asked.

Ben was puzzled. 'Jake, you have come into this shop and asked for many things, but I never expected that you would one day ask for a Bible.'

'We need it,' said Eliza. 'It is part of our plan to save the jetty.'

'In that case, I wish I could help you, but a Bible I do not have.'

'Do you know where I could get one?' asked Jake.

'Try the church, but I doubt they would let a kid take one away. Haven't you got a Bible at home?'

'Mum would kill me if I took our family Bible,' said Jake. 'It is very old and has all the family's marriages recorded inside the front cover.'

The kids left Ben's shop wondering what to do, but then good fortune stepped in. Miss Brown was looking in a dress shop window, and she was Jake's number one authority on matters pertaining to the Bible. They marched up to her. 'Hello, Miss Brown, do you know anyone around here who could lend me a Bible?' asked Jake. Then he waited for her reply, unsure how she would react. Their last conversation had ended with her in tears, but fortunately, all appeared to have been forgiven.

'Good heavens, Jake,' said Miss Brown. 'You would be the last Sunday School student I would ever expect to ask me that question, but it is wonderful to see you taking such an interest. However, I must ask, why do you need one now?'

'We need it to save the Old Jetty,' said Jake.

'I don't understand,' Miss Brown replied.

'Ask Eliza, she knows.'

'It is very hard to explain,' said Eliza, 'but we are about to ask the kids on the Town Jetty to be believers. Their voices are needed if we are to save our jetty from destruction.'

I couldn't have put that better myself, thought Jake, and Miss Brown was equally impressed.

'Oh my,' she said. 'What a wonderful idea. I believe that we could have saved many things from the ravages of storms had we prayed in advance for their protection. I will go with you, and we can all pray together.' She reached into her handbag and pulled out what appeared to be a tattered notebook. 'I always carry this little Bible with me,' she said. 'It was given to me by my grandma when I was just a girl.'

'Er, we are not going there to pray,' said Jake.

'Take me to your friends, and we will talk about the rest later,' said Miss Brown.

'Okay.'

The three marched onto the jetty, which puzzled the kids who were all about to go home. Jake seldom missed a morning's fishing, but he had recently missed several. His sudden appearance made them curious, and they wondered why he had a girl and his Sunday School teacher with him. Fortunately, everyone other than Boof, assumed that the girl was a friend of Miss Brown, which saved Jake from being given the *Jug's got a girlfriend* jibe.

The kids were gathered close to a seat which Eliza thought would make an excellent podium. 'Hop up there and talk to them,' she said to Jake.

'I don't know anything about protests,' he replied. 'You have to explain that bit. I will bribe them with Ferris wheel tickets once they know what they have to do.'

'Okay,' said Eliza, but her voice was uncertain. She was in the camp of the enemy and about to ask for their help, and it would be the first time that she had ever made a speech of any kind. With great trepidation, she hopped onto the seat and took a deep breath. 'Can I have everyone's attention please,' she shouted, and then she paused, for she had surprised herself. She was talking in a strong voice that she never knew she had, and she already had their attention.

It is amazing how easy it is to get people's attention when you are wearing a yellow hat, thought Jake.

Eliza continued. 'Jake and I are organising a protest to stop them demolishing the Old Jetty,' she said.

'That is a lie,' Hoppy shouted.

Jake became angry. He was not going to let Hoppy call Eliza a liar. He jumped onto the seat and shouted, 'Hoppy's dad has put up a fence to close the Old Jetty and has told us that it is about to be demolished.'

'Who cares,' shouted Hoppy. 'We can catch all the fish we want on this jetty.'

'I bet you don't catch salmon,' said Eliza. 'Jake and I caught a big salmon off the Old Jetty the other day.'

'So that is how you got blood on your shirt,' shouted Boof.

'Yes,' said Jake, 'and if Hoppy hadn't started this stupid jetty war, some of you would have been catching salmon there as well that day.'

'You are a traitor,' shouted Hoppy.

'No, you are the only troublemaker,' growled Jake. 'The Old Jetty kids would like to be friends, but you stopped that happening when you threw that bike in the water. And you are a coward as well, because the Old Jetty kids know that if they fight a town kid, your old man will sack their dads.' Jake was no longer worried about Cassidy retribution and had come out with all guns blazing.

'No, you are the liar,' said Hoppy. 'Dad told me that the jetty has been closed for safety reasons.'

'I can prove that I am telling the truth,' said Jake. 'Miss Brown has her Bible with her, and I will swear on it.'

Miss Brown pulled her Bible out of her bag, upon which Hoppy went into Cassidy mocking mode.

'That could not be a real Bible,' he laughed. 'It looks like a grubby notebook that most people would have thrown in the rubbish bin by now.'

Miss Brown was a person who loved the world and all things in it, but something inside her clicked. That Bible was amongst her most cherished possessions, and she read it every day. With anger welling inside of her, she jumped onto the seat. 'This certainly is a real Bible,' she shouted, 'and Jake and Eliza are organizing a protest to be held outside the town hall at three this afternoon. I would like you all to be there.'

Then Jake added, 'Everyone who comes gets a free Ferris wheel ticket.'

'Yea, let's do a protest,' the kids all shouted.

'Wonderful,' said Miss Brown, 'and perhaps we should say a little prayer for God to be with us.'

Jake cringed. *I think she is starting to get a bit carried away,* he thought, but Eliza shouted, 'Why not. It won't do any harm to have God on our side.'

To Eliza's surprise, no one opposed her opinion. They bowed their heads while Miss Brown said a short prayer. It was a strange ending to what had been a strange event. An event that had given Miss Brown a new respect for her wayward Sunday School student, while at the same time giving the student a new respect for his teacher.

38

THE PROTEST

It was shortly after three that afternoon when the mayor's secretary walked into his office. 'Excuse me, Mr. Mayor, but there is a bunch of kids protesting in front of the town hall.'

'Is that the noise I can hear?'

'Yes, and they are a somewhat rowdy group if I may say so.'

'Tell them to go away or I will call the police.'

'But their Sunday School teacher seems to be their leader.'

'Surely not Miss Brown,' said the mayor. 'She would never get caught up in a protest.'

'She is there alright, and I never realised until now, that she has such a loud voice.'

'But what would she be protesting about?' asked the mayor.

'Something to do with the Old Jetty, I think.'

'Oh, is that all,' the mayor replied. 'I know about that problem, and all will be remedied at tomorrow night's council meeting. I will go out there and put their minds at ease.'

The mayor strode onto the stairs of the town hall.

'Save the Old Jetty,' chanted the kids.

The mayor raised his hands. 'Quiet please and let me tell you that no harm will come to the Old Jetty. The council will be ordering the removal of the fence at tomorrow night's meeting.'

An egg came flying over the crowd and splattered on the mayor's shoe. Jake turned around. 'Want to throw an egg?' said Boof, 'I brought a whole basket full of them.'

'Did you not hear what the mayor just said?' growled Jake.

'No, but I got him first shot. I bet you can't do that.'

Miss Brown raced up to the steps and stood beside the mayor. 'Stop, everybody. Throwing eggs is no way to protest. We are here to use our voices only.' Then she turned to the mayor. 'Sorry, Mr. Mayor. I had no idea that was going to happen.'

'That's alright,' said the mayor. 'Fortunately, I appear to have none on my clothes. My wife would be so upset if she had to take this suit back to the dry cleaners so soon after last time.'

'Perhaps a kind angel saved your clothes,' said Miss Brown.

'I don't know about that,' said the mayor. 'I think if a kind angel had been involved, the egg would have missed me altogether, but I do admire the passion the kids have for saving their jetty.'

'Let's go to the Ferris wheel and get our rides,' Jake shouted, then he frowned at Boof who was about to throw another egg. 'Put down your egg,' he growled.

Jake could see that only harm would come if they continued the protest, but he was still worried that the mayor would be doing nothing until after the council meeting.

Everyone headed for the Ferris wheel where they enjoyed a ride much longer than normal, but it was Miss Brown who enjoyed it the most, for she had found a cause for which she could make a difference. Councillor Cassidy's power was impacting on the town's children, but their parents were afraid to act because they feared Cassidy retribution. It was therefore up to her to help their kids fight a cause that would benefit everybody.

Meanwhile, Jake and Eliza rode once more in their yellow chair, but both shared Ben's concern that demolition of the jetty would start before the council had its meeting. 'We have to stop them working their tomorrow,' said Jake.

'Perhaps we could organise a picket line like the ones the workers do,' Eliza suggested.

'Good idea,' Jake replied. 'You can ask Ivan to bring his gang and I will ask Miss Brown to bring the Town Jetty kids.'

'What will you be doing?' asked Eliza.

'I will ask Ben for padlocks and get there early,' said Jake. 'They won't be able to start work if we padlock their stupid gate.'

Once the ride was over, the protesters gathered beside the Ferris wheel where Jake laid out his plan for the next morning.

39

BOTTLES' LAST STAND

It was not long after midnight, that Bottles was woken from his slumber. A truck had just driven over the top of him. He opened his eyes, reached for a torch he kept by his bed, then flashed it around the room. The beam caught the face of a laughing clown.

Bottles staggered to his feet, wondering why anyone would drive a truck onto the Old Jetty in the middle of the night. He opened the door to his bunker, making sure that no light spilled to the outside. That long forgotten bunker had been his secret haven for years. It was the only place he felt safe; a place where he could retreat from the world, but it would lose its feeling of safety if people were to learn that someone lived there.

He climbed onto the jetty and discovered that the offending truck had backed up to the wire fence. He listened and heard voices, then crept up to the vehicle. It was a council truck, laden with tins of kerosene and several boxes marked, *Explosives*.

A strong smell of kerosene filled the air. *Surely, they are not going to set fire to the jetty,* he thought, but what other conclusion could there be? The men in the truck had walked to the far end of the jetty and were soaking the planks with kerosene.

He stepped back into the darkness because the men in the truck were returning, then he watched as they swapped empty tins for full ones. 'We have to work faster,' said one of the men. 'Cassidy wants this place ashes by sunrise.'

It appeared that the men were going to spread kerosene from one end of the jetty to the other, and soon all would be ablaze. Bottles had to stop it, but how? He could not talk and there was no time to run for help. The place would be ablaze by the time help arrived.

He returned to the bunker and picked up the phone, then dialled the only number he knew, hoping to hear the friendly voice of his brother.

His brother was Bottle's lifeline. Unknown to most, Bottles could speak, but only his brother ever bothered to interpret the mumbled words that came from his broken mouth. Making others understand was an embarrassment, so Bottles would just say, 'Ug.'

Unfortunately, his brother did not come to the phone, which left Bottles with only one choice. He would have to make a citizen's arrest, knowing that his brother would come by in the morning. He grabbed his revolver and went back to the truck, where he removed the ignition keys. Then he waited in the shadows for the firebugs to return, and when they did, he stepped back into the light. The men jumped in fright, and then gasped upon seeing the gun. 'What do you want, Bottles,' asked one of them.

Bottles gestured that they get into the truck, which they did, thinking that they might escape by driving it away. However, they soon discovered that the keys were gone, and what Bottles did next, made their blood run cold. He placed a box of dynamite on the truck's bonnet and aimed his gun at it.

'Don't shoot,' came a shout from inside the truck. 'If you do, this truck will explode like a five-ton bomb.'

Bottles nodded, then he sat on an empty kerosene tin he had placed a safe distance away. His citizen's arrest was now complete, the prisoners trapped in the truck, thinking that Bottles had gone mad. 'We had better do as he says,' one said to the other, 'or he will probably blow us up.'

Only Bottle's brother knew that Bottles was the town's most decorated war hero, lost in a raid behind enemy lines. Originally thought to have been killed in an explosion, the Red Cross had found him in a hospital sometime after the war. They had arranged for him to return to his hometown, but Bottles could never face the one he loved. He thought that returning from the dead in such a sorry state would be unfair to her, so he let people continue to believe that he was dead.

Biggles was Bottle's brother, and he had promised to always look after Bottle's welfare, but to do this, he had to remain in the town. He had asked Councillor Cassidy to use his influence to make sure that he was never transferred. In return, he agreed to do whatever the councillor wanted, but the councillor never knew the reason for Biggles' request.

A few days earlier, Bottles had called his brother because he had cut his ear, and his brother had come to his aid. However, in their haste to leave for the hospital, they had left the bunker door open, and Jake had gone in and found blood on the phone. But Biggles could not come to Bottles' aid that night, because the councillor had sent him on an overnight errand. He wanted Biggles out of town while the jetty burned.

As the night drew on, a cool wind began to blow, so Bottles took more kerosene tins and built a small wall to shelter behind. Then a car drove up the jetty, stopping when it reached Bottle's tin wall. Councillor Cassidy was at the wheel, wondering why the jetty was not yet ablaze. What he found, had him confused. Only the truck's cabin was visible above the tin wall, and in it he could see his men, sitting in the truck when they should be working. He wound down his window and shouted, 'This is no time for a tea break, you loafers. The blasting team will be here tomorrow to get rid of whatever is left.'

Then he saw Bottles' head pop up from behind the wall. 'What are you doing here, Bottles?' growled the councillor, but he said no more when Bottles waved his gun. The tyres squealed on the councillor's car as it retreated in reverse.

A short while later, police headquarters received a phone call from the councillor. 'There is a maniac on the Old Jetty,' the councillor reported, 'and he is holding my men at gun point in a truck loaded with explosives.'

This was not the type of phone call the police superintendent ever wanted to receive. He called in the special operations team, including a sniper, all of whom were still in bed. Once assembled, the team left headquarters. 'Make sure the press does not hear about this,' the superintendent told the staff as he left. He did not want reporters at the Old Jetty, thinking that his sniper might have to shoot a mad man.

Back at the jetty, Bottles was guarding his prisoners when he heard a siren. A vehicle with flashing red lights came racing along the esplanade, then stopped at the start of the jetty. Next, the beam of a search light lit up the truck, but Bottles stayed hidden behind the tin wall.

'Give yourself up,' shouted the superintendent. 'We have a sniper with orders to shoot if you make one false move.'

Bottles did not answer, but the men in the truck saw the danger. 'Don't shoot,' one yelled through the truck's open window. 'A stray bullet could blow this whole place apart.'

The superintendent saw the problem and turned to one of his men. 'Take the wagon and get us some breakfast,' he said. 'This looks like being a long siege. We could be here all day.'

But the councillor needed the siege to end right then, because he only had a few hours left before the council would meet and take away his authority to destroy the jetty. 'You have to end this siege now, even if it means shooting the maniac,' he said. 'He's only the town bum and no one is going to miss him.'

The superintendent was shocked by the councillor's callous attitude. 'Sorry, but there is far too much paperwork involved if we do that,' he said, trying not to show his sudden dislike for the councillor. 'I am looking to have a peaceful settlement here.'

'You have to shoot him now, before he shoots someone or blows up the truck,' the councillor argued.

The superintendent ordered a rope to be stretched across the entrance to the jetty. 'No one steps beyond the rope without my permission,' he said, 'and that includes you, Councillor.'

It was just before sunrise when Jake arrived with his padlocks, but he soon found that they were not needed. 'Stop,' shouted the superintendent as Jake went to step over the rope. The shout caused Bottles to pop his head over the tin wall.

'Now is your chance to shoot him,' shouted the councillor, and he pointed towards Bottles.

Jake thought he had walked into a situation only ever seen at the pictures, but it was real. The Old Jetty, the place kids came to fish every morning, had become the scene of a standoff between the police and a baddie hiding behind a makeshift barricade.

'Who is behind those tins?' Jake asked the councillor.

'Bottles,' came the angry reply. 'He has gone mad, and this useless lot have just missed a chance to shoot him.'

Jake had never seen a picture show where good guys shot at good guys, because that would make no sense to the audience, but he could see it happening in real life. He was only a twelve-year-old kid, but in that moment, he saw himself as the sensible one surrounded by adults who had no idea what they were doing. He ran towards the tin wall because he had to warn his friend. 'Keep your head down,' he shouted upon getting there, but Bottles already knew the danger.

Bottles nodded and pointed to the men in the truck, the boxes of dynamite, and the tins of kerosene. But he did not have to point out the gun in his hand, because that was what Jake saw first. He had seen that gun before and guessed that Bottles was the man who lived in the bunker.

'He is holding us at gun point,' shouted one of the men in the truck.

'Why?' asked Jake.

'I don't think he wants us to set fire to the jetty.'

'Why are you doing that?'

'We work for Councillor Cassidy, and he told us to do it.'

Meanwhile, the superintendent thought that he now had an extra hostage to worry about. 'Why would that stupid kid have done that?' he growled. 'That's going to be more paperwork. I knew I shouldn't have volunteered to do the early morning shift today. Thank goodness there are no reporters here.' But the words had barely left his lips before another car arrived. It was the professor, and with him were the gentlemen of the press.

40

THE GANGS UNITE

The professor had to call in a few favours to have a reporter and photographer come to the Old Jetty at that time of morning. They were hoping to capture the arrival of a demolition team but would have preferred to still be in bed. However, their attitude changed when they saw the special operations team and a police sniper. A page five story about seahorses losing their home, was suddenly a front-page scoop that could be worldwide news by teatime. Excited, they went to hop over the rope, but the superintendent stopped them.

'Is there a gunman behind those kerosene tins?' shouted the reporter.

'Yes, so get back or you might get shot.'

Jake heard the superintendent's words and realised that the police thought that Bottles might start shooting people. 'I must tell them it is not a siege,' said Jake, but Bottles shook his head.

Jake thought for a moment and then realised that the siege was the only thing stopping the men from burning the jetty, so he sat down beside Bottles.

However, the siege was about to enter a new phase, for Eliza arrived with the Old Jetty Gang. 'This is a police siege operation and you kids have to leave immediately,' shouted the superintendent, but the kids were going nowhere.

They began chanting, 'Save our jetty.'

The superintendent waved his hands in the air, because he did not have enough men to implement crowd control. 'Okay, you can stay,' he said, 'but don't cross over the rope.'

Then Miss Brown arrived with the Town Jetty Gang, further adding to the superintendent's crowd control problem. He stood in front of the throng of kids and repeated his order. 'No one must cross the rope,' he bellowed, but then Jake stepped out from behind the tin wall.

163

'Come out here and join us,' he shouted. 'Bottles has caught two men trying to burn down the jetty.'

The Kids made a rush in Jake's direction, and the superintendent was powerless to stop them. He tripped and fell while getting out of their way, but Miss Brown stopped and helped him back to his feet.

'Thank you, madam,' said the superintendent. 'I am sorry that you had to witness such shocking behaviour on your morning walk.'

'I am not at all shocked,' said Miss Brown, and then she raced out to join the others. The superintendent was left speechless.

Miss Brown joined the kids and told them to form a picket line in front of the tin wall, but her arrival had the men in the truck bewildered. Being held hostage by a gun toting Bottles who had a handkerchief hiding his face, was like something only seen in cowboy westerns. It was weird, but when a pack of kids joined the cowboy bandit, it got weirder. However, none of this could equal the shock they got when their old Sunday School teacher joined the fray. That was the icing on the cake.

'Jake, what is going on here?' asked Miss Brown.

'Bottles stopped these men from burning the jetty,' Jake replied. 'He thought he was making a citizen's arrest, but it seems that the law is not on his side. Tonight's council meeting will fix everything, but we have to stop these men until then.'

Miss Brown looked at the men in the truck, and then everyone heard her angry voice. 'Clifford, William,' she said. 'What would your mothers think if they knew that you were about to set fire to your town's most historic jetty? Do it, and your names will go down in infamy.'

The men looked at each other and then at Miss Brown. She was glaring at them, the same as she had glared at them whenever they had mucked up at Sunday School. They had to choose. Do they stay with Councillor Cassidy, keep their jobs, and be on the side of evil, or do they join Miss Brown, keep their mothers happy, and have the town's history record them as being on the side of good. They chose the Miss Brown team. 'What can we do to help?' they asked.

'You need to stay here and pretend to be hostages,' Miss Brown told them.

'For how long?'

'Probably until the council meets tonight.'

'Okay,' said one of the men, 'but that is a long time. Do you think you could organize some food for us?'

'Good idea,' said Miss Brown, and then she shouted to the superintendent, 'Could we have thirty hot pies and a case of cold soft drinks please. We are all getting hungry.'

'Starve them out,' cried the councillor, but the professor thought otherwise.

'I will get the goodies,' he yelled, and then he hopped into his car and drove away.

Miss Brown turned her attention to Bottles. She had seen him walk past her house almost every day, but she had never been this close before. There had been times when she would have liked to have said, 'Hello,' but he had always walked away before she reached him. She knew he could not speak, but with the handkerchief around his face, and the floppy brimmed hat that he always wore, people only ever saw his eyes. She looked at his eyes and saw something familiar. Without knowing it, she said, 'James?' which was the name of her fiancé who never came back from the war. Bottles turned his back, and so she found herself saying it again. 'James, is that you?'

Jake had never heard Bottles laugh, cry, or say anything other than, 'Ug.' But in that moment, he heard him begin to sob. Miss Brown went over and put a comforting arm around him.

Jake thought about the picture he had found in the bunker. Could it be that Bottles had once been Miss Brown's boyfriend? The men in the truck were thinking the same, for the whole town knew that Miss Brown's heart had been broken when her war hero fiancé, James, never came back from the war.

'Hey, kids,' said one of the men. 'Why don't you go for a walk up the jetty and give Miss Brown and Bottles some privacy.'

'Are you coming with us?' asked Jake.

'We can't. We have to stay here and pretend to be hostages, so we will just close our eyes.'

The men in the truck now knew what was happening, but the superintendent still had no idea. In his experience, hostage takers usually shout their demands while bystanders keep their distance, but this hostage taker was yet to utter a word and the bystanders were running amuck. Fortunately, the bystanders had now left the scene and were walking up the jetty, but even that made no sense. Councillor Cassidy had asked him to shoot the hostage taker, telling him that he was a maniac, but that made no sense either.

'Can you tell us what is happening?' shouted the reporter.

'I have no idea,' replied the superintendent, but Councillor Cassidy was becoming furious.

'This situation would never have developed if these incompetent police officers had done their job properly when they first got here,' he said.

'You mean like shooting the man holding the hostages?' asked the reporter.

'Precisely.'

'Can we quote you on that?'

'Yes.'

The photographer took the councillor's picture while the reporter scribbled the conversation into a notebook.

It was then that Biggles arrived on the scene, having returned from his overnight errand. He thought he had been delivering papers needed for a court hearing that morning, but it was just a ploy set up by the councillor to get him out of town that night. 'What is happening here?' he asked.

'The town bum is holding hostages in a siege and Councillor Cassidy thinks we should shoot him,' said the reporter.

'What town bum?' asked Biggles.

'Bottles,' snapped the councillor.

'Bottles is not a bum. He is a war hero,' shouted Biggles. 'He just wants people to leave him in peace. If any harm comes to him, I will make such a fuss that even the Prime Minister will hear about it.' The reporter scribbled down every word, and then came a voice from behind. The professor was back.

'Can someone give me a hand with these goodies,' he said. 'They are for the protesters out on the jetty, and I got there just as the bakery opened. The pies are hot, and the drinks are cold.'

Biggles and the professor carried the pies while the reporter and photographer carried the drinks, all of which further confused the superintendent. Everyone was ignoring his instruction to stay behind the rope, and this latest group had a fellow police officer with them. 'Stop,' shouted the superintendent. 'I am in charge of this police operation. Where do you think you are going, Officer?'

'We are taking them to my friends up the jetty,' replied Biggles.

'There is a man behind that tin wall, and he has a gun,' said the superintendent.

'That man is my brother,' Biggles growled, 'and the gun can no longer shoot bullets. It's a war souvenir and I personally disabled it myself.'

'But he is staging a siege.'

'My brother can't speak,' said Biggles. 'If he could, I am sure he would tell you that what is happening here is simply a peaceful protest. Please let us deliver what they want.'

The superintendent shrugged. 'Go ahead,' he said. 'You have convinced me. I just want to know exactly what it is that is going on here.'

The men in the truck were the first to see a tray of hot pies coming their way. 'Hey kids, the pies are here,' one yelled from the truck window. The kids came running back.

Then Biggles found his brother in the embrace of the woman who was still officially his fiancé. *Thank goodness*s, he thought. *They have finally found each other. Perhaps he will now realise how silly he has been all these years.*

It had been an odd situation where Biggles had watched over Bottles, while at the same time, Bottles had watched over Miss Brown.

Bottles felt it was better that she thought he was dead, for he did not wish to burden her, but he still wanted to make sure she was safe. When Jake and Eliza had pasted a circus poster over her Sunday School sign, he had been quick to tear it down. At times, Miss Brown would wonder who had left fruit on her doorstep, or how broken things in her yard got fixed, but she had never thought of Bottles as being the culprit.

Biggles walked back to the superintendent accompanied by the two former hostages. 'You might as well pack up and go,' he said. 'I have impounded the truck because it is an offence to drive explosives through a town without a permit.'

'Are you going to press charges?' the superintendent asked the men.

'No way,' one of them replied. 'Bottles is a hero, and we would never cross a picket line.'

'But Councillor Cassidy said you were being held at gun point?'

The man shrugged. 'That was a misunderstanding. Bottles never pointed that gun at anyone, he just waved it around as a way of making people understand him.'

'But Councillor Cassidy said he was dangerous and that we should shoot him,' said the superintendent.

'In this town, shooting Bottles would be like shooting Bambi,' the man replied.

The superintendent frowned at the councillor, then said, 'I think you need to come with me. There are some things I would like to sort out with you back at headquarters.'

41

HOW IT ALL ENDED

What happened that morning was to change the town forever, and the first of those changes had its beginnings in the interview room at police headquarters. There in were sitting the superintendent and Councillor Cassidy, and both men had a problem. The superintendent had a report to write, but he was not sure what it was that he was reporting on. The councillor had said it was a siege, but everyone else said it was a peaceful protest. The councillor had also asked him to shoot the man behind the tin wall, and if it were only a protest, then the councillor should be facing serious charges.

The superintendent thought about the kids and their protest, and they reminded him of kids he had come across during the war. His battalion had been entering a small town it had taken a few days before, when he passed a group of kids dressed in tennis whites. They were lined up along the roadside, tennis racquets in hand, and had come for their regular game of tennis. However, what they found was a large crater in the middle of what was once the town's only tennis court, and they were waving their tennis racquets in anger. The superintendent could still remember the look on their faces, and their faces were flashing back to him that morning, for the kids on the jetty were the same. They were lined up in protest because they were losing their jetty, and the jetty was all that they had. No one had ever provided them with tennis courts, or anywhere else to play for that matter. He decided to put a proposition to the councillor.

The councillor could either defend a charge of attempted murder that the superintendent was prepared to lay, or he could pay for tennis courts and a recreation hall to be put on the Workers Village Sports Field.

When the town council met that night, it had much to consider. First was the matter of the Old Jetty, which they declared a marine sanctuary due to its colony of Seadragons. It was never to be demolished. Then they considered the matter of the men who had tried to set it on fire. They were declared blameless and kept their jobs, because they had been acting under Councillor Cassidy's instructions. Finally came the matter of Councillor Cassidy. The mayor asked him if he wished to speak prior to the council removing him from all positions he held.

The councillor rose to his feet and asked for forgiveness. He told them that the events that morning had given him a new respect for the town and its people, particularly the new arrivals in the Workers Village. As a result, he was going to pay for the establishment of tennis courts and a recreation hall to be built on the Workers Village Sports Field.

The councillor kept his job and went on to be one of the town's great benefactors, and never again did he use his power to bully people. Always, he was mindful that the gentlemen of the press and several others were keeping his dark secret, for they were the ones who knew how he had once asked for the town's greatest war hero to be shot.

Ben also benefitted from that day, for he no longer had to worry about being put out of business by a competitor. Far from it, for he was soon to have a new partner, and they opened an entirely new and very successful business. It began with a sign that appeared in Ben's window, right alongside of the one advertising maggots. The new sign read, *Get Your Broken Wireless fixed by the Wireless Wizard.*

The venture flourished, and people came from miles around to get their wirelesses fixed. The electronics wizard who made it all happen, had to give up his old job, which meant the council had to find someone new to drive their rubbish truck. However, he always kept in contact with his friends at the dump, because that was where he got most of his spare parts.

A year later, Ben and his partner moved into new premises, for TV was coming. They named their business, "The Wireless Wizard", and it was among the first to sell and repair television sets. From time to time, Jake's dad would drive past their shop, and he would feel proud that his son was such a good friend of the Wireless Wizard's daughter.

Eliza's dad, alias the Wireless Wizard, also kept up his weekly game of chess with his good friend, Bottles, and they formed a chess club. Biggles was one of the club's founding members, for he was also a keen player. It was the regular games of chess that he had with his brother when his brother lived in the bunker, that had sharpened their chess playing skills.

But it was the lives of Miss Brown and Bottles that changed the most. With the aid of speech therapy, surgery, and a neat beard, Bottles was once more confident to face the world. They married, and Biggles was their best man. In his speech he told how his brother had written a book of love poems devoted to his bride, and how he kept the book in a chest by his bed. He also told of a time when the circus had come to town. A mother had shamed him because he had stopped her son from putting up circus posters, and in an act of conscience, he had asked his brother to help him put the posters up that night.

Jake always said that the day of the Old Jetty Protest was the most important day in the town's history, for that was the day that the jetty war ended, and enemies became friends. Councillor Cassidy's sporting facilities were built not long after, and they brought everyone together. Soon, the town was fielding teams in sports previously ignored by the locals, and many of the town's first sporting heroes came from the families of the new arrivals. Ivan was the town's first junior tennis champion.

In the years that followed, the diversity of nationalities grew, and the town's main street became known for cafés that offered cuisines from many parts of the world. At the same time, festivals started happening on the foreshore. These colourful events would attract visitors from far and wide, and people would celebrate with music, dance, food, and even the flying of kites.

However, there was one event that held a special meaning to many. The town would hold an annual ball in the Workers Village Sports Field Recreation Hall to commemorate the day of the Old Jetty protest, and a highlight of that evening was the fox trot. That was when everyone would take to the dance floor to honour Miss Brown, the town's unassuming Sunday School teacher who had led the protest.

Ben had once said to Jake that it was up to his generation to bring their divided community together, but Jake did not know what to do about it. However, the process had already begun, because a girl in a yellow hat had chosen to give a perceived enemy a pair of bike valves.

***

Jake sat in his living room, thinking back to happenings now sixty years in the past. He recalled the last day of his holidays, hoping to see Eliza just one more time before boarding the train back to school. He recalled how it was Violet who had come to see him off that day. She had handed him a note from Eliza, explaining she could not be there because she was in bed with the measles. But it was how the note was signed that had struck him the most. There was no signature, no words to say who had written it, just a small love heart drawn at the bottom.

Jake still had that note, and on occasions he would bring it out. He would recall how the girl that had delivered it, had gone on to marry Eliza's brother, and Hell had not frozen over despite some saying that it would.

Suddenly, Jake heard a voice from the kitchen, bringing an end to his mood of nostalgia.

'Jake, when are you going to fix this tap?' said the voice. 'If you don't fix it soon, I will have to get someone else to do it.'

'Got any particular person in mind?' chuckled Jake.

'Gorilla Boy,' laughed Eliza. 'That is, if the circus ever comes back to town.'